NBC Great ESCAPES

TRADE WINDS

Created by Hugh Bush
Written by Janet Quin-Harkin

Schoolfield/Caribbean Productions of the
Cramer Company in Association with
NBC Productions

ISBN: 0-812-53658-4

A Tom Doherty Associates Book
in association with
A Creative Media Applications Book

10 9 8 7 6 5 4 3 2 1

Printed in U.S.A.
First printing, August 1993

Created and written for television by:	Hugh Bush
Opening two-hour episode directed by:	Charles Jarrott
Executive Producer:	Douglas S. Cramer
Producer:	Hugh Bush
Producer (Opening Two Hours):	Mary Catherine Harold
Unit Production Manager:	Christopher Seitz
Casting:	Jackie Briskey
Director of Photography:	Isidore Mankofsky
Production Designer:	Roy Amaral
Set Decorator:	Linda Sutton
Costume Supervisor (Opening Two Hours):	Tom Baxter
Makeup:	Sheri Short
Hairstylist:	Kareen Boursier
Origination:	Filmed on location in St. Martin-French West Indies and St. Maarten, Dutch West Indies
Produced by:	Schoolfield/Caribbean of the Cramer Company in Association with NBC Productions

STARRING:

Efrem Zimbalist, Jr. as Christof Philips
Anita Morris as Lafetita Gabetti Philips
John Beck as Robert Philips
Michael Michelle as Maxine Philips
Michael McClafferty as Ocean Sommers
Stephen Meadows as Rick Sommers
Barbara Stock as Grace Sommers
Dean Tarrolly as Joseph Gabetti
Ned Vaughn as Anthony Philips

ALSO STARRING:

Rebecca Staab as Ellen Sommers
Allan Dean Moore as Kyle Philips
Sam Hennings as Will Philips
Claudette Roche as Marigot Philips
Kim Hamilton as Madame de Gaulle
Paula Trickey as Nurse Topping
Lindsey Ginter as Hugo Rotterdam
Gregory McKinney as Duncan Laurant
Randi Ingerman as August de Gaulle

TRADE WINDS

See all the characters and locales come to life in the NBC mini-series, filmed entirely on the Caribbean island of St. Martin!

And you're really going to enjoy NBC's new fall lineup! It's filled with more passionate dramas like "Trade Winds," plus touching family dramas like "Sisters" and "Against the Grain." You'll find sexy comedy, sophisticated comedy, crazy comedy! And they shine with many of your favorites, because the stars are back on NBC!

SISTERS

Returning for its 4th season, this is an acclaimed series about families as they really are—fighting, loving, caring, ready to do anything, go anywhere, for a sister.

AGAINST THE GRAIN   NEW SHOW!

A father follows his dream, and takes his family with him. This new series about life in a small all-American Texas town makes you feel good about who you are and what you're doing.

MAD ABOUT YOU   NOW ON THURSDAYS!

Voted "Best New Comedy of the Season" by the Viewers for Quality Television, "Mad About You" now joins NBC's Thursday night lineup for the greatest night of TV on TV!

𝒯HE MOMMIES `NEW SHOW!`

They're neighbors who share the pains and the (sometimes) pleasures of motherhood—they're real moms, they're real funny! Starring one of the hottest new comedy duos in the business.

𝒞AFÉ AMERICAIN `NEW SHOW!`

Valerie Bertinelli returns in a sparkling new comedy! She's a young woman who chucks it all and runs away to Paris in search of romance and excitement . . . only to discover that there's a waiting list for romance and excitement.

𝓔MPTY NEST

This "empty nest" just keeps getting more crowded, more crazy. There are two great new additions to the cast: Marsha Warfield, from "Night Court," and Sophia herself, "Golden Girl" Estelle Getty!

𝒩URSES

Loni Anderson returns to series TV as a hospital administrator. She joins the group of hardworking nurses who are so good with their patients, and always good for a laugh.

 NBC

CHAPTER 1

The speedboat cut through an ocean as smooth as glass. The water was so clear, every movement of swaying seaweed, every dart of a small reef fish could be seen on the bottom, forty feet below. Christof Philips noted with his fisherman's eyes a school of yellow jack hanging motionless above the coral, the settling of a peacock flounder, and the graceful wing flap of a large ray. For a second he wished he'd brought his spear gun along, but he quickly put fishing from his mind. Today he was after bigger game than fish. Today he was going to prove if his secret theory was correct.

Now in his mid-fifties, Christof was ruggedly fit and youthful looking. He was a big man with that characteristic German square jaw. His face was weathered from years of sun and sea, but it was a handsome face that women still found attractive. Having worked hard all his life, his body was well muscled.

Christof's sons had inherited his good looks. Robert, his older son, had his father's square jaw and the strength that had made him a star linebacker for his American prep school. Will's taller and slimmer frame allowed him to excel in sports requiring agility and speed. He was lethal on the tennis court and was currently representing his college at basketball. Christof thought fondly of his sons. He was glad that Paradise Rum had prospered enough for him to send them to American schools and after that to American universities. Better to be an American in this world than a German. Americans were likable and liked. They made money and minded their own business. They didn't become two fanatics, the way his countrymen seemed to. Christof couldn't stand fanaticism. While a student at Freiburg University, he had protested loudly against the growing madness of Hitler, and had been forced to leave his country rather than face a concentration camp.

After a long odyssey, during which he had changed his name from Von Philips, then met and married Ingrid Braun, a fellow German refugee, he had finally settled on the island of in St. Martin. The place suited him: half French, half Dutch, with no border between the two halves. It was Christof's idea of how society should be run. Everybody got along. French and Dutch settlers could buy land in each other's territory. Islanders and Europeans could sit and drink together. Police turned a blind eye to the back-alley cockfighting. The Catholic chaplain was used to voodoo priests turning up at baptisms and funerals to provide their own form of blessing. Time didn't matter and the outside world, with its menace of war, was only a rumor on a very distant horizon.

Christof and Ingrid had prospered on St. Martin. A small sugar cane farm had developed into a large rum empire. Christof's taste for good rum had encouraged him to start making his own brews, and one thing had led to another. Now Paradise Rum was exporting crates to the States and the rest of the world as fast as the stuff could be bottled. Christof nodded with contentment. He had everything he wanted—and at last, some leisure time. Time to pick up on his long lost interest in his studies: naval history in particular. He had begun charting the voyages of the Spanish fleet and one particular wreck caught his eye. *La Targa*, a Spanish galleon laden with a cargo of gold from Colombia, had reputedly sunk off the coast of St. Kitts in the 1600s. Many diving expeditions had been launched, but no trace of the ship had ever been found. While out in his boat fishing one day, Christof had been struck how alike the shape of the two islands were. This coast could almost be St. Kitts … which opened up a fantastic possibility. Perhaps the sunken galleon wasn't lying off St. Kitts at all—she was here, off St. Martin.

The edge of the reef loomed ahead—a clear line where the water changed from turquoise to deep cobalt. Christof cut the motor and the sleek mahogany boat drifted into silence. He threw out the anchor and waited until it caught bottom before he started to put on his scuba gear. Usually he didn't go diving alone. Ingrid didn't like him to take chances. "What if you get into trouble? Who would save you?" she'd ask in the clipped German accent she had never managed to lose. "Who would take care of me and the boys if you were gone?"

But today he didn't want any prying eyes around. Even Dante, his trusted chauffeur who usually accompanied him in the boat, had been left behind. If anything too spectacular was brought up from the wreck, he knew that Dante wouldn't be able to resist bragging. There were no secrets on an island only thirty miles across.

Christof strapped on his air tank and slipped his feet into the fins. It was a perfect day for diving. The sun shone from a cloudless sky. In the distance, blue sea merged with blue sky on a smooth line of horizon. Back on the island the sun reflected off windows dotting the slopes of the Pic du Paradis, the island's shaggy mountain peak. A fishing boat left Marigot harbor but it headed toward St. Barts, as he knew it would. He felt alone and powerful. Nobody could stop him in this quest. If he succeeded, he would be wealthy beyond his wildest dreams. But it was the historical discovery more than the wealth that lured him: he already had almost everything he wanted—a loving wife, two fine sons who would one day take over the business, and a lifestyle that would have been impossible if he had stayed in his native Germany. How many of his fellow students back in his fraternity at Freiburg now had their breakfast brought to them on a tray by a slender bronze girl with a hibiscus flower in her hair? How many breakfasts included fresh papaya and hot French bread delivered from the bakery? How many of them had a stable of horses, a powerboat, a sailboat and a fishing boat, a private plane, the freshest seafood at their doorstep, and the smoothest rum ever made by man? "Paradise," Christof muttered to himself with satisfaction as he turned his gaze back from the island to the open sea and his quest. It might be nice to be wealthy beyond his wildest dreams, but what he really wanted was the satisfaction of proving he was correct. He'd write a paper about it for an important journal. He'd put his treasure on display. Archaeologists from around the world would come and admire what he had brought up from the depths.

Not too deep, he hoped! It would be crazy to dive too deep alone. If anything happened and he had to surface in a hurry, it could be fatal. But if the records were accurate, then *La Targa* had not slipped down into the abyss. She had been stuck fast on the reef, her main mast above the breakers, her crew hopelessly looking at a shore they couldn't reach while they died of saltwater madness. Christof slipped on his mask and adjusted the fittings. No sense in taking chances just because he was eager. If he had an accident with his equipment today, there would be no Dante to rescue him. For a moment he wished that one of his sons were there to share the adventure with him. Will would have gone with him, although Will preferred dry land to the ocean, and he found Will hard to talk to. Will didn't seem to like talking much to anybody. He was happiest on his own, out with the dogs or horses, going through the sugarcane fields. Robert would have been interested in the intellectual challenge, and he would have come to please his father, but Christof got the impression that his older son preferred his books to a day on the water.

Rick Sommers would have come like a shot, Christof thought with a sudden stab of regret. Why was it that he got along so well with the neighbors' son, and he felt so awkward with his own two boys? Unlike them, Rick seemed to delight in sailing, and he loved to admire the beauty of the island—and its women. In fact, he loved life.

There was a certain charisma about Rick that drew people to him. Christof had already noticed the way the young girls clustered around Rick at parties.

He's going to have trouble with women later in life, Christof thought with a smile. He knew what that sort of trouble was like. He was a ladies' man himself. But if Rick had been there now, Christof thought, his face would be glowing with excitement. He'd be fiddling impatiently with his own equipment, itching to get down into the sea. If Christof actually discovered the wreck and he was still diving when the boys came home from college, he'd take Rick down with him.

He put in the mouthpiece, then sat on the side of the boat and fell backward into the water. Instantly he was aware of being in another world. Even though he had made hundreds of dives, he never failed to experience the same thrill of freedom as he moved effortlessly through the water. It was the closest thing to flying he could imagine, his body suddenly weightless, no direction impossible. Down and down he went. The bottom was quite sandy with only lone rocks and banks of coral rising up from the ocean floor. At first the area seemed devoid of life, but as he approached a large staghorn coral, a school of brilliant blue angelfish darted across his path and an inquisitive sergeant major fish swam right up to his mask. Usually they made him laugh with their fearlessness—four-inch fish taking on a six-foot man—but today he brushed them aside in his impatience.

Christof reached the area he had selected from studying the maps, and started sifting through the sand. He had passed over the spot a few times before and convinced himself that a pattern of coral outcroppings could, in fact, be the ribs of a ship. Down there it was harder to tell. As he dug into the sand, the water became cloudy. Then the sand settled back in the same place. Not a very efficient operation. He'd have to come up with something better if he found evidence that this was indeed the site.

All I want is one small sign, he thought. One cannonball would do it, one piece of pottery, anything. He picked up a hard round object, then recognized it as a shell and discarded it in disgust. Curious fish had come to join him. The sergeant majors were back, hovering in front of his mask again, making it hard to see. A barracuda swam past him, looking with cold yellow eyes to see if his digging had unearthed any interesting prey. He glanced up for a moment, then went back to his work. His long association with barracudas had taught him that they were dangerous only if you held a spear with a struggling fish on it. Then they were apt to miss the fish and bite you instead. But it did remind him of the danger of sharks. One very good reason for having Dante up in the boat was that he could be on constant lookout. The area was not known for its dangerous sharks, but one could never tell.

He worked on, moving along the coral, digging and probing into crevasses. The sun, shining through fifty feet of water, reflected off what looked like the top of a small tin can. He bent to scoop the object up and found he was holding a large, perfectly intact gold coin.

Almost immediately a shadow passed overhead. He looked up, startled, to see a good-size lemon shark drift

BUSH/ QUIN-HARKIN

over him. The lemons were not normally dangerous, but he took it as an omen and prepared to come to the surface. He had found what he wanted—proof that a Spanish galleon had foundered there. Now all he had to do was establish that this ship was *La Targa* and start digging!

It was mid-morning when he tied up at the Marigot pier. In the square beyond the harbor, the market was in full swing. Christof walked past wizened old women sitting behind little piles of breadfruit and plantain, palm baskets from which live chickens squawked plaintively, flying fish in neat rows on a marble slab, a lobster waving helplessly with string-tied claws. Usually it gave him pleasure to observe all this, to feel himself part of the pulse of island life, to listen to the lilting Creole sounds, the steel drums, the guitars, and the lively arguments which belonged on any Paris boulevard. But today he hardly noticed what was going on around him as he pushed his way through the crowd.

He wasn't aware of the old man until he almost ran into him. Then Christof looked up, expecting the old man to step out of his way. He was used to being known and recognized on the island, and most natives deferentially stepped aside. But this man didn't move. He was so old and weathered that his face resembled a wrinkled prune. Christof noted right away he wasn't wearing European clothes. Instead, the man was draped in dark-colored robes that seemed to overpower the frail body beneath. On his head was a sort of headdress of black feathers and beads, and he carried a stick in one hand. He held the stick up to Christof, blocking his path. Christof could feel the skin prickle at the back of his neck.

——— 14 ———

"What do you want?" Christof demanded harshly to hide the irrational fear that was mounting in his throat. "I have no money on me."

The old man's eyes flickered. "Yes, you have money," he said in strongly accented Creole French. "Yes, you have much money."

It suddenly struck Christof that the man knew about the coin. He couldn't explain how, but the man knew.

"Who are you?" Christof demanded. "What do you want from me?"

"To warn you." The old man continued to stare until Christof felt his heart laboring in his chest.

"Go away. Leave me alone," he said, "I want nothing to do with you or your stupid voodoo nonsense." And he started to move back through the crowded market square. When he looked back over his shoulder he could see the black robes behind him. He got the absurd notion that death was following him, and he began to run, heedlessly pushing people out of his way. Every time he glanced over his shoulder, the black robes were still flapping behind him. He could hear exclamations and curses as he knocked over a stall, but he didn't stop until he was on a quiet back street behind the square, where he could double back to his parked car.

When Christof tried to start his car, he found that his hands were shaking. "Voodoo nonsense," he muttered to himself, but he suddenly felt cold. He must have stayed in the ocean too long. A good swig of rum would warm him. He owned a little beach hut just out of town, where they sometimes had parties. There would be a bottle of rum waiting for him there! He drove to the hut and hurried inside, amazed at the way he locked the door behind him. Really, he was behaving quite irrationally for an educated man! What could an old voodoo priest do to him? Voodoo worked only on superstitious natives. Besides, he had done nothing wrong. He was known for his good relationship with the islanders—surely he hadn't offended any voodoo God. He took a long swig of rum, feeling the warmth spreading throughout his body. As the rum worked on him, he found himself relaxing, lying back contentedly on the old rattan sofa. Pure imagination, brought on by being underwater too long.

The light tap on the door made his heart leap violently. At first he decided he'd keep quiet and pretend he wasn't there, but then he remembered his car was parked outside.

"What do you want?" he called fiercely.

The lock slid back, the door began to open, and the old man came in. His robes blocked the bright sunlight from the doorway.

"What do you want with me?"

"To warn you, before it's too late," the old man said. "To tell you that you must not go back."

"Go back where?"

"To the ghost ship," he said. "Let it be. Do not disturb the ghosts, or they will have me do their bidding. They will make me take others to join them. Others close to you. Those closest to you."

"Who are you?" Christof demanded, his throat so dry that he could hardly speak. The air was heavy with the smell of fear.

The old man mumbled something in a language Christof couldn't understand, then said clearly in French, *"Je suis le docteur de la morte."*

"Doctor of death?" Christof muttered. "What do you mean by that?"

But the old man had gone.

By the time Christof drove up to his house, his fear had almost vanished. He approached the secure front gates and honked for the boy to let him in. In the distance, the rambling stucco house stood among manicured lawns dotted with flowering trees and shrubs. Bougainvillea made a flaming trail across the porch. He let out a sigh of relief as he drove up the gravel driveway and parked by the front porch. This was his home, safe, normal, European—away from all that primitive island nonsense. He felt ashamed that he had let the old man get to him. He was sure that the old man was genuine and meant what he said—there were many voodoo priests on the island—but voodoo was for islanders, not immigrants from Europe. He had never believed in ghosts before, so why should he start now?

He ran his fingers through his hair as he ran up the steps into the house.

"Ingrid?" he called, waiting for her to come running.

"The missis is not feeling too good," a voice behind him said. He hadn't heard her coming, but Madame de Gaulle stood there, eyeing him with that sharp, penetrating gaze of hers that always made him feel uneasy. It was as if she could read his thoughts. He had a brief moment of panic that the illness had been caused by the old witch doctor.

"What's wrong with her?" he asked sharply.

Madame de Gaulle shrugged. "Just a slight cold. Nothing to worry about. She was asking for you." She looked at him pointedly again.

Christof wondered why he always felt like a schoolboy when facing his housekeeper. He was, after all, the employer and she the employed, but it never felt that way. He had to admit that Madame de Gaulle was remarkable. She was a striking-looking woman with smooth ebony skin and that wonderful proud bearing of the islanders. She looked as if she feared nothing, which was probably true. Her dress always bordered on the outlandish and Christof was sure she did it for effect. Even her name was outlandish: She claimed a wartime liaison with the famous French general, which nobody could actually prove or disprove. Most people were inclined to believe it was true: How else could she have acquired all those mementos that turned her house into a shrine for the old general? There was even one of his uniforms framed on the wall. She also had a daughter of the right age, with a certain European look to her. Anyway, nobody disputed her colorful past, and she ran the household like clockwork, as if she, not the Philips family, owned Plantation House.

"I was out in the boat," Christof said, feeling he must account for his whereabouts.

"Oh, yes? You go fishin'?"

"Right. A spot of fishing."

"You catch anything?"

"No. Nothing worth keeping anyway."

"Oh," she said, and continued to stare. "That's funny," she went on in her lilting speech. "I thought you catch somethin' pretty special."

"What are you talking about?" he demanded uneasily. He was remembering that Madame de Gaulle was also rumored to have inherited voodoo powers from her mother.

"I just thought you might have been meddling where you'd no business to be meddling," she said.

"I haven't got time for women's gossip," Christof said, "I've got work to do." He started to move away.

"Don't turn your back on island warnings," she called after him sharply. "That ship is full of hungry ghosts. Let it lie."

"What are you talking about?" he demanded. She couldn't possibly know. Nobody knew except him!

"I'm talking about the ghost ship that went down on the reef," she said. "It came to rest on the bottom and the poor sailors climbed up into the crow's nest, safe above the waves. They could see land, you know, but not one of them tried to swim ashore. And you know why? They were afraid to leave all that treasure to the others. So what did they do? They slowly starved to death. They went mad from drinking seawater and ate each other until they were all gone. All because they wouldn't leave the treasure."

"How do you know all this?" Christof asked shakily. He had found it out from the oldest of books stored in a Miami archive.

"We know," Madame de Gaulle said scornfully. "It's our history, isn't it? We know our own past and we respect it, we learn from it. You should too, if you know what's good for you."

"Huh," Christof said. "Superstition. Too much superstition on these damn islands."

He ran up stairs to his bedroom. Ingrid was lying in bed. Her eyes were closed and she looked so peaceful that Christof was terrified for a moment that she was dead.

"Ingrid, *Liebchen?*" he said.

She opened her eyes and smiled at him. "Why Christof, you're back. I wondered where you were."

"Just out and about," he said. "How are you?"

"Just a little under the weather. Nothing serious," she said. "You know how I get these colds in the winter."

"You should have a change of climate," he said. "This house gets damp when it rains. That's not healthy."

Ingrid sat up. At forty-five she was a lovely woman with long blond hair spilling over her shoulders and hardly a sign of a wrinkle. Her eyes were a clear light blue and they sparkled when she was excited. "Why Christof, that's a marvelous idea," she said.

"What is?"

"Let's go away for a while. The Hamiltons have been begging us to come visit them on St. Barts. We should take them up on it. I understand they've done wonders with their estate. Effie Hamilton's even put in a fountain. It's supposed to be just like Versailles."

Christof's eyes lit up. "We could try out our new plane."

"To St. Barts?" Ingrid looked wary. "What's wrong with the boat?"

"Takes too long. What's wrong with the plane?" Christof demanded. "What's the point of having a plane that we never seem to use?"

Ingrid frowned. "I don't know that I like the idea of fly-ing to St. Barts, Christof. That airport is supposed to be the most dangerous in the Caribbean."

"Only in bad weather," Christof said, "and I wouldn't be flying it myself. Nick Thomas is a good pilot. I wouldn't have hired him otherwise."

"All right. So we go by plane if it makes you happy," Ingrid said. "And we could ask the Sommerses to join us," she went on. "They've been working so hard at that hotel, Christof. All those troubles with the builders and then the setback with the hurricane last year: It's not easy to get a new hotel going."

"They just need patience," Christof said. "It's a very attractive building and the site is spectacular. If they can just get it on its feet, it will be a very desirable property."

"And you'll double the rent on the land, you old scoundrel," Ingrid said, patting her husband's hand.

"I might buy back the hotel if it starts doing too well," he said with a wink.

"Christof, what do you know about hotels?" Ingrid said.

"I knew nothing about rum, but I seem to be making a go of that," he said. "Don't worry, Ingrid. We'll let the Sommerses sweat it out trying to make Trade Winds prof-itable and I'll stick to my Paradise Rum."

"So what about flying to St. Barts?" Ingrid insisted. "Can I call Mary Jo and ask them to come along? You like talking with Pete, don't you?"

"Oh, yes. Pete's a good man," Christof said. "I enjoy the Sommerses' company. Now, if Rick were here …."

"Oh, you and Rick," Ingrid said, shaking her head in

amusement. "I do believe you prefer him to your own sons."

"We seem to be on the same wavelength," Christof said. "I've nothing against my two, but they seem to take life so damn seriously. They must get that from you!"

"They'll need to take it seriously when they have to run your business one day," Ingrid said. "And I imagine that Rick Sommers will sober up a little when he has to take over Trade Winds. I don't imagine that hotel will ever be a piece of cake to run. So when can we go, Christof? Can I call the Sommerses?"

"Hold on there," Christof said, putting a restraining hand on her. "I thought you were supposed to be sick. We'll go someday soon, I promise, but right now I'm all tied up with cane cutting."

"Oh, Christof," Ingrid said, "that's what you always say. You're always too busy to take your wife anywhere."

Christof bent and kissed her head. "Soon, *Liebchen*, I promise. Very soon," he whispered, and tiptoed out of the room. He had planned to go directly back to the factory and see how the fieldwork was coming along, but his hand closed around the coin in his pocket. He was struck with how cool and smooth and heavy it felt. Surely it couldn't hurt to identify it—just to put his mind at rest as to what he had found? He glanced around to make sure Madame de Gaulle was out of sight before he entered his study and locked the door. He took down a large tome on artifacts of the early Spanish period. This was the definitive source of diving archeology. Christof flicked through it impatiently. When he came to the page on coins, he took the coin from his pocket and placed it on the table. Two dolphins with tails intertwined and the initials *N.R.* Christof knew that those initials stood for Nuevo Rieno de Granada, today's Colombia. His excitement growing, he began to run his finger down the page. Then he ran his finger down the next page and the next: There was no coin like it in this book. He had discovered a new coin. He knew from experience that this alone would be worth up to ten thousand dollars. If there was a whole shipload of such coins … Christof's heart began to pound.

That night Christof dreamed he was diving. The water was so clear that he could pick out every pebble and shell hundreds of feet away, almost as if he had magnified vision. He was swimming over coral and suddenly a voice said, "Down here, you idiot. Don't you see?" And when he looked, he could see perfectly the outline of a boat. There were cannon sticking up through the coral and neat piles of gold bars glinting through a fine layer of sand … He woke, his heart pounding. He had to go back down once more. He just had to see if he would recognize the spot as he did in his dream!

The next morning when Ingrid woke, she found him already up, staring out of the window.

"What is it, *Liebchen*?" she murmured. "It's awfully early, isn't it?"

"Going to be a beautiful day," he said. "I've been think-ing. You do need to get away. Why don't we call the Sommerses and pop over to St. Barts today. Take a picnic. It should be a lovely flight."

Ingrid leapt out of bed and flung her arms around his neck. "What a wonderful idea," she said. "I'm going to call Mary Jo this minute and tell her we'll be over to pick them up around eight."

Christof began to feel guilty as he watched her bustling around the house, buzzing with excitement. They drove to pick up the Sommerses and then headed for the tiny airport on the French side of the island. Ingrid and Mary Jo chatted happily all the way, wondering if they had packed enough food and whether what they were wearing was suitable for visiting the Hamiltons at their newly refurbished home. Pete and Christof exchanged amused glances.

"You'd think we were heading for Buckingham Palace," Pete commented.

When they reached the airfield, Christof helped load the picnic baskets onto the plane, then he assisted the Sommerses on board and kissed Ingrid.

"What's this? You're not coming?" she asked.

"There's a couple of things I need to check on first," he said. "You can send the pilot back for me."

"Oh, but Christof, you promised," Ingrid said, her face a picture of disappointment.

"I'll be over later. I promise," he said. "Go ahead and have a good time admiring the Hamiltons' fountain."

He closed the door and the plane taxied for takeoff. He watched them as they soared up into the sky. Then he drove furiously down to the harbor. The water was rougher than the day before as he sped out to the site. There was a stiff breeze and clouds raced across the horizon. No wonder

Ingrid had felt under the weather. Her head was a superb barometer of approaching storms! He had to work fast: It was hopeless trying to dive deep if the sun wasn't shining. You couldn't see a thing. He yanked on his mask and shoved in the mouthpiece before tumbling into his silent world below.

He was sure that he had anchored in exactly the same spot, but after swimming up and down for half an hour, he had seen none of the features he recognized from the day before. Where was that big staghorn coral with the angelfish? The bottom lay before him smooth and undisturbed, as if a storm had been through and left everything neatly rearranged. Damn, he thought. He started sifting though sand anyway, but after an hour he still hadn't found anything.

Serves me right, he decided. I should have gone with Ingrid like I said I would. Oh well, the wreck isn't going anywhere. I can always come back another day ....

When Christof surfaced he saw that storm clouds were already gathering on the western horizon—a solid bank of dark gray that contrasted with the blue sky above it. "That will put a damper on Ingrid's picnic," he said. He turned the boat for home and sped in across waters that faded to pearl as clouds covered the sun. As he stepped ashore he glanced up, half expecting to see the old voodoo doctor waiting for him, but instead he noticed his head clerk, Laffite.

He sprang up the last of the steps. "Is something wrong at the factory, Laffite?" he demanded.

He could read the fear in Laffite's face. "Oh, M'sieur, the

call just came through ... we didn't know where to find you."

A white-coated official stepped past him. He recognized Jean Hetreau, the chief gendarme.

"I'm very sorry, Mr. Philips," he said in strongly accented English. "I regret being the one who has to tell you this."

"Tells me what?" Christof demanded. "My factory? Has something happened?'

"Not your factory, M'sieur," the policeman said. "Your wife. There was a sudden storm, you see. The plane struck the mountaintop while trying to land ...."

"Is she ... going to be okay?"

The policeman shook his head. "Oh, no, M'sieur. The plane caught fire. There were no survivors. I'm very sorry ...."

Christof turned away, trying to comprehend this. As he looked along the harbor wall, he saw the old man standing there, his black robes billowing out in the wind.

CHAPTER 2

The three young men, Rick Sommers and Robert and Will Philips, arrived on the island on the same plane, two days later. As Christof waited for them on the tarmac, he didn't know how he would have the courage to face them. Making the phone calls had been hard enough. But at least that task had been made easier by the extreme distance and static on the phone lines. All three boys had hardly said a thing anyway. He imagined they were in shock, just as he was. He had gone about his tasks as if in a dream from which he would soon wake. He refused to believe his wife and friends were dead, that he would never see them again, never stroke Ingrid's hair or hold her in his arms or make love to her … it all seemed so impossible.

He was grateful that he had such an efficient staff around him. It was Lafitte who attended to all the details of death certificates and the funeral. It was Madame de Gaulle who planned the funeral banquet and decided who they should invite. It was a long list. They knew everybody on the island and Ingrid was well liked. "Don't worry about a thing, M'sieur Christof," Madame de Gaulle said. "We'll take care of it. My daughter is back home now and she can help me. You need time alone with your grief." And from the way she looked at him, that hard, penetrating stare, he was sure that she was reproaching him the way he was reproaching himself. "You did this," her eyes were telling him. "You brought it on by your pigheaded stubbornness. We all warned you, but you wouldn't listen."

Christof sighed. It was too late now for regret. Nothing he could say or do would bring them back to life. He watched the Fokker Friendship land, its propellers whining noisily, and he let out a sigh of relief. He had half expected this plane to go up in flames as well. Ground crew wheeled out steps and the door opened. He watched impatiently as American tourists stepped out, squealing with delight as they took in the shaggy green mountains and the blue Caribbean sparkling in the distance. The three boys were the last to come through the door. Christof realized with a jolt that he always thought of them as boys, and yet they were all young men. Even Rick, the youngest of the three, was now twenty-one. Robert was four years older. Christof thought back wryly to when he was twenty-five. He had already seen enough of life to make him grow up in a hurry. He had escaped from the Nazis, tried his hand at many professions in many countries, married, started a sugarcane farm and had his oldest son. Maybe this tragedy would force these three to grow up in a hurry.

Robert stepped ahead of the others and blinking in the strong sunlight, looked around. He was dark-haired like his father, broad shouldered, and had the strong, straight features that Christof had possessed as a young man. His hair was immaculately groomed and he looked every inch a young, successful executive-to-be. He was wearing a dark suit, which Christof was sure he hadn't owned before. Trust Robert to always do the right thing, he thought. Will, in contrast, was still in jeans and T-shirt. Lankier and a couple of inches taller than his brother, he had his mother's slim features and light eyes. And Rick … Christof stared at Rick as the boy stood at the top of the steps, his strawberry-blond hair blowing in the strong breeze. Usually Rick reminded him of a young Nordic warrior, blond, bronzed, muscled, but today he looked as if he hadn't been to bed since Christof phoned him. His eyes had a hollow, haunted look, and he hadn't shaved or combed his hair in days.

He was the one who spotted Christof first and waved. Christof hurried forward and threw his arms around the boy. "Rick, my dear young friend. I am so sorry. ." he said in a cracked voice. "I can't tell you how sorry I am."

"You might take a moment to comfort us too, Father." Robert's voice came from his shoulder. "We have just lost our mother, you know."

Christof looked up into the solemn face of his oldest son and then into Will's bewildered eyes. "Of course I try to comfort you too," he said. "We try to comfort each other. I've just lost my beloved wife. The woman I loved more than anything in the world …." He had to stop as he choked on the last words. "But poor Rick has no one now. I know how he must be feeling." He put his arm around the young man's shoulder. "You come back with us to the house. I don't want you to have to go back to Trade Winds alone yet."

"Thanks, Mr. Philips," Rick said. "I was dreading going home to an empty hotel."

Robert glanced at Will as they walked to the car.

The funeral was as beautiful as Ingrid had been. The weather was mockingly bright and clear. Flowers bloomed in riotous profusion, spilling over mausoleums and family vaults, and hummingbirds whirred around the hibiscus. From the ocean nearby came the squeals of children at play. It was as if the whole world were in contrast to the somber event. Christof found that he was watching passively, like a spectator—as if the mahogany box being lowered into that hole in the ground had nothing to do with him or his life. It was impossible to believe that it contained his wife and he would never see her again.

He found it surprisingly easy to play the good host, to shake hands and thank people for coming, just as if it were one of his famous parties and not his wife's funeral. He found himself warmly inviting everyone back to the house.

"My housekeeper has prepared a fabulous spread, I'm sure," he said. "She's famous for her langoustines."

He drove back with Rick and the boys in his car.

"I thought that went pretty well, don't you?" he said, trying to ease the silence with conversation.

"I suppose so," Robert muttered. "I've never been to a funeral before, so I have nothing to compare it to."

"Did you notice the old voodoo priest standing behind the tamarind tree?" Will said, his face breaking into its accustomed grin. "I was dying to see if he would step forward and take part in the ceremony. I'd love to have seen Father du Bois's face if he'd had to interrupt his prayers for a little voodoo."

He had meant to lighten the mood, but his father spun

around. "What voodoo priest?" he demanded.

"Didn't you see him up on that grassy area where the tamarinds are?" Will asked. "He was standing there all the time. Had one of those impressive sticks in his hand."

"I didn't see him," Robert said.

"Me neither," Rick agreed, "although I wasn't looking around much. I just couldn't believe it was happening. It didn't seem real somehow."

"I know what you mean," Robert said with sympathy. He leaned across to Rick. "What will you do now, do you think?"

"Give the boy a chance. He just got here," Christof said.

"I just wondered if he'd given it some thought," Robert retorted. "If I were in your shoes, Rick, I'd sell up while the getting was good and make a real life in the States. You wouldn't get much out of the hotel, but enough to finish your studies."

"Maybe I don't want to go back to the States," Rick said. "Maybe I like it better here."

"Agreed, it's much nicer here," Robert went on, "but from a practical point of view, your parents put everything they had into building that hotel and they never really got it to turn a profit. There's no way you can build it up by yourself."

"But I still want to give it a try," Rick said. "As you said, Rob, my parents slaved over that hotel. They put their life savings into it. I wouldn't want all their hard work and dedication to be for nothing. I think it's up to me to carry on with their dream now, and that's what I intend to do."

"And what will you do for money?" Robert asked.

"I understand they've a small accident insurance policy," Rick said. "That should get me started. I guess I'll do the rest with my own two hands. I can patch roofs and paint ceilings and I've got ideas too. You wait, Robert. In a year's time you won't know Trade Winds. You'll have to make a reservation a week in advance to come over for lunch."

Robert laughed good-naturedly. "I hope you do make a go of it, Rick," he said. "I wish you all the luck in the world."

"What about you two?" Rick asked. "Will you go back to finish school?"

"Of course they will," Christof boomed. "I haven't paid for all those years of expensive education so that they can quit before they've got the degrees in their hands."

"It's not the same for us," Robert said. "We're both in our last year. Will is working on his agricultural degree and I should get my MBA. Between us, we'll be well qualified to turn Paradise Rum into the biggest business in the Caribbean."

"We'll send Robert out to persuade everybody in the States to drink rum instead of beer," Will quipped. "Can't you just see at baseball games—Get your ice cold rum punches here?"

"And all the commercials on TV when the men sit around a campfire drinking rum and saying it doesn't get much better than this?" Rick added.

They were all laughing by the time the car drew up at the Philips house.

Madame de Gaulle greeted them at the front door. "Everything's ready, sir," she said. "I think I've done you proud. Champagne to drink—that always lightens the mood, and food that's not too heavy or rich—shrimp mousse, a cheese board, some langoustine with mayonnaise, plenty of fruit."

"Sounds wonderful, Madame," Christof said. He went to pat her shoulder, then thought better of it. "I hope we have enough. There were a lot of people at the gravesite, and I seem to have invited them all."

"We always have enough," Madame de Gaulle said with dignity. "Why don't you come along through to the dining room and I'll get Dante to serve the champagne?"

As they started through for the dining room, Christof touched Rick's arm. "Just a moment, Rick. If you'd just step into my study."

Rick followed Christof through a side door into a book-lined room. Carefully Christof closed the door behind him.

"I feel very bad about this whole thing, Rick," he said. "I'd like to make it up to you somehow."

"It wasn't your fault, Mr. Philips," Rick exclaimed. "It was a horrible accident. Nothing could have been done to prevent it."

"But it was my fault," Christof blurted out. Rick looked at him strangely. Christof shrugged. "I suggested the whole thing. I told Ingrid to go. I invited your parents to go along with us. It was my plane. I should have been on board. I changed my mind at the last minute."

"At least we have one thing to be thankful for," Rick said. "Just think what your boys would be going through now if they had to take over Paradise Rum as well as mourn for their parents."

Christof put a hand on Rick's shoulder. "You're a good boy, Rick," he said. "I've always liked you. I'd hate to lose you as a neighbor, and I want to do what is right."

He went to the filing cabinet and opened a drawer, taking out a slim folded piece of paper. "I want to give you the deed to your land," he said. "I want Trade Winds to be completely yours, free from worry about paying rent."

"Mr. Philips," Rick stammered. "I hardly know what to say. It's the best site on the island. Are you sure?"

"I'm sure, Rick," Christof said softly. "It would make me feel a whole lot better if you'd take it."

Rick pushed the paper away. "It's very generous of you, but I can't accept."

"It's only right, Rick," Christof said. "Take it to please me. Think of it as a way to make me feel better about this whole horrible business."

"Well, all right, if you insist. Thank you," Rick said.

"Good boy," Christof said. "Only promise me one thing. This must remain a secret between us. I don't want my boys to know that I've given you this. They already feel I favor you too much. It would create bad feeling."

Rick frowned. "They're going to find out sometime."

"Then I'll tell them when I'm good and ready," Christof said. Now would not be the correct time. So I have your word on this that you'll say nothing about it?"

"Of course, Mr. Philips," Rick said. "I just hope it doesn't cause any problems later on."

"Why should it?" Christof snapped. "Our business is rum, not hotels." He clapped a big hand on Rick's shoulder. "Now, we'd better get out there before the hungry hordes arrive."

Robert was hovering nearby. "What was all that about?" he asked as Rick walked ahead to the dining room.

"Just a friendly little talk," Christof said. "I just wanted to make sure the boy was all right."

"I hope you didn't give him money," Robert said.

"I thought Rick Sommers was your friend?" Christof said. "You two were always together when you were younger."

Robert frowned. "I like Rick, Father. He is my friend, but family is family. You've always been rather soft where Rick's concerned, and it occurred to me that if he can't make a go of the hotel, we might just acquire it back."

Christof put an arm around his son's shoulders. "Stick to rum, Robert," he said. "It's been good to me and it will be good to you. And don't begrudge anything I do for Rick Sommers. I owe him a debt you can never imagine."

"For what?" Robert asked.

But Christof couldn't tell him. He had a horrible suspicion that his son would laugh at the idea of a voodoo curse. There was no way that Robert or Will would ever understand that he had caused those deaths, actually been responsible for all of them. He was very glad he had decided to say nothing about the deed to the Trade Winds land. He had a feeling that his boys wouldn't understand about that either. If and when they found out, he'd make it seem like a legal maneuver. Perhaps the deed had been forced out of him in an out-of-court settlement by Rick's lawyer? Yes, that was a good idea. It made sense. That's exactly what he'd say.

Will had gone ahead into the dining room. Everything

looked so perfect: the crisp white tablecloth, the large flower arrangement of hibiscus and bird-of-paradise in the center, the polished silver serving dishes, the gleaming crystal. It reminded him of all the parties of his childhood, all the Christmases and New Years and Bastille Days and birthdays. His mother had loved to entertain. Usually at this stage she would be bustling around nervously, straightening every napkin for the tenth time and exclaiming at intervals that nobody would come and they'd have all this food to eat up. Of course everyone did come and the party was always a success. It was impossible to believe that his mother was no longer there to hover over the table, making sure that guests didn't die of starvation. He glanced up as he sensed a figure standing in the shadow at the far end of the room. For a moment his heart flipped over, as if his mother's ghost were standing there. But then he saw it was someone quite different: a tall, slim black girl with flawless skin and big, dark eyes. Her hair was cropped close to her head, and tucked above her ear was perched a scarlet hibiscus. She was wearing a simple white dress that fitted her like a glove, accentuating her small, firm breasts and neat waist. The skirt had a slit up one side, revealing a slender thigh, and she was barefoot, which explained why he hadn't heard her enter the room. Will thought she was the most lovely thing he had ever seen.

"Hello, Will," she said in a smooth, deep voice with almost no trace of accent. She walked across the room to him, her bare feet seeming to glide over the polished floor. Then, as he didn't answer, "Aren't you going to say hello?"

"I'm afraid … I mean I'm not sure that I …." he stammered.

The girl laughed. "Surely you remember me, Will Philips," she said. "I'm Marigot."

"Marigot? Madame de Gaulle's little girl?" Will exclaimed. "The scrawny little kid I used to have swimming races with?"

"And I always beat you," Marigot replied with a delighted smile that revealed perfect white teeth.

"But you've grown up so much," he said, realizing as he said it how stupid it must sound.

"You've grown a little yourself," she said, her eyes traveling up his six-foot frame and giving every indication that she liked what she saw. "It must be years since I saw you last. It must have been when you were first sent away to that boarding school. You were a skinny kid then. I could beat you at wrestling too, if I remember correctly. I bet I couldn't beat you in a wrestling match now." She moved so close to him that her breasts almost brushed against him. Her eyes challenged him and flickered in delight when he blushed.

"So what have you been doing with yourself, Marigot?" he asked. "You haven't been around the last few times I've been home."

Marigot grinned. "Being turned into a lady," she said. "I was at a convent on Antigua."

A look of alarm shot across Will's face. "You're not thinking of becoming a nun."

The girl gave a delighted peal of laughter. He thought she had the most joyous laugh in the world. "A convent school, Will."

"But I thought your mother was involved in voodoo!" Will blurted out before he realized that this was another ridiculous thing to say.

Marigot laughed easily. "*Maman* thinks the more gods you have in your pocket the better," she said, "and besides, there are no voodoo schools where you can learn good manners and how to do embroidery."

"Is that what you learned at the convent?"

She looked at him, her eyes sparkling. "I spent most of my four years on my knees in the chapel asking for forgiveness," she said. "I was always caught running in the halls and talking during silent hour. The nuns were glad to see the last of me. And I them," she added.

"And after school?"

"I've been working at a hotel, over on Puerto Rico," Marigot said. "Perfecting my English and learning about Americans—mostly how to dodge groping American hands. *Maman* thinks they are two useful skills."

"But you're back home now?" he asked. His face betrayed his expectancy.

"I might be," she said. "I haven't decided yet what I want to do long-term. I might stick around for a while. How about you?"

"I've got four more months until I graduate," Will said. "Then I'll be back here for good."

The room was filling up with guests. Will hardly noticed as they moved around him. He couldn't take his eyes off Marigot for a second. "Do you think you'll stick around that long?" he asked boldly.

"Marigot? Where is that child? " Madame de Gaulle's

voice came from the doorway. "I've got hot food getting cold in the kitchen," she said pointedly.

Marigot gave Will a dazzling smile. "I might," she said, then she darted off through the crowd. Will gazed at the doorway after she had vanished. He wanted her desperately.

CHAPTER 3

The taxi bumped along the rutted driveway leading to the Trade Winds hotel. The taxi was an ancient Studebaker, quite unsuited to the hairpin curves on St. Martin. A sticker on the windshield proclaimed that it was air-conditioned, which was untrue. A fan blew with a lot of noise, but didn't actually produce any cold air. Rick Sommers was glad of that. He loved the feel of the island breeze in his face, the constant taste of ocean salt on his lips, and the stickiness on his bare skin. It made him feel that he was truly back home again. At college in Wisconsin there had always been an artificial climate: central heating that was way too hot in the winter and air-conditioning that gave him perpetual colds in summer. He wouldn't miss Wisconsin, he thought. He was annoyed that he wouldn't get his degree, but he wouldn't miss the place. It had been an interesting experience to play at being an American again, but he knew that he didn't belong there. He couldn't get passionate about football, and the girls all seemed too pale and phony. His pulse quickened as he thought about warm island girls, tanned skins, small bikinis, and the hot moonlit nights that seemed to melt away inhibitions. It was easy here to have as many women as he wanted, but so far none of them had meant anything more to him than a few hours' pleasure. Now suddenly he wasn't a college kid anymore. He was a man who owned a hotel, and a future in the "real world" lay ahead of him. He wondered if he would ever find a woman who could be to him what his mother was to his father—companion, coworker, friend as well as lover.

The taxi swung around a bend and Rick's throat tightened as he saw the familiar imposing façade of the hotel. Seen from this distance, it was most impressive: built in the gracious island style with a cool, pillared entrance way opening onto a central courtyard full of luxuriant palms and shrubs. Beyond a backdrop of palm trees the ocean sparkled and glittered. Situated in the middle of a white sand beach, protected by cliffs at either end, fronting on a yatch habor, it was the center of its own private world.

"Is this place still open?" the taxi driver inquired. "I don't seem to drive nobody up here."

Rick was tempted to say that his sort of guests usually rode up in one of the newer taxis, but instead he said, "Yes, it's open. It hasn't been doing too well this year. That last hurricane was bad publicity."

The taxi driver nodded agreement. "Though it hardly touched us at all. I understand they show the islands all blown away on the American television. Was the hotel get damaged?"

"I think the roof was slightly damaged, and of course some of the lawns were destroyed by the high waves, but nothing major. All we need is a little word-of-mouth advertising to get us on our feet: So any time someone asks you for a recommendation, bring them here, and you'll get a commission from me."

"From you?" The old man laughed.

"That's right," Rick said. "I'm the owner." As he said it, he felt a rush of pride and power. Since receiving the shocking news of his parents' death, he'd felt only a hollow emptiness. He didn't believe the feeling would ever go away. But suddenly he found himself looking forward to the future. He would make a go of this place in spite of what everyone said. He'd make it into the jewel of the Caribbean. The most influential people would fight to book rooms at Trade Winds. He would make his parents' hard work pay off.

The taxi screeched to a halt and Rick got out, leaving the driver a generous tip. Always useful to have the island taxi drivers on your side. The man saluted and drove off. Alone for the first time, Rick stood in the shade of the columned porch. Now that he was this close to the hotel, the glamorous vision had faded into reality. Only ten years old, the salt had already begun to eat away at the white stucco façade and the sun was blistering and fading the green paint on the shutters. The gardens ran wild, and Rick suspected that the staff hadn't done a thing since his parents' accident. There was definitely to be done! Rick walked up the steps and into the hotel.

Old Dumas looked up from the front desk as he walked in. "Welcome home, Mr. Rick," he said. "My deepest sympathy. I wish you could have come home to happier times."

"Thank you, Dumas," Rick said. He looked around,

taking in the empty lounge. "So what is happening? Do we have any guests at the moment?"

"The last ones left when they heard of your parents' tragedy, Mr. Rick, and I was told to cancel all bookings until we knew what was going to happen to the place."

"How many bookings was that?" Rick asked.

"Seven or eight, I believe."

Rick winced. The loss of seven or eight lots of guests was crucial to a hotel that had never yet been full.

"What's going to happen is that I'm taking over Trade Winds," Rick said. "Would you please assemble the staff and ask them to meet me in the lounge in fifteen minutes. I've got some things I want to say."

Rick felt his pulse racing, and his throat tightened as he faced his new employees. He knew his parents had had trouble with them. They would smile and agree with everything they said, and then do everything exactly as they pleased. Rick knew he had to make them more productive, or else the hotel would fail. But how would they react to being given orders by someone they considered a mere college boy? He had to gain their respect to start with or there would no sense in carrying on. He let his gaze sweep over them and smiled.

"Bonjour," Rick began, trying to sound more in control than he felt. "I have good news for you. Trade Winds will remain open. Nobody will lose their jobs in the near future. I will be staying in St. Martin to run it. I expect everything to be in condition to receive new guests tomorrow. I noticed that some things have been neglected since my parents' accident. The lawns need mowing. Our front

lawn is a great asset to this hotel, not to mention the impression a guest will have. Are you in charge of that, Claude? Good, well, see that it's taken care of this afternoon, will you? And Dumas, I'd like to do a complete inspection. When we're through, we can talk about long term maintenance."

Yes, M'sieur," Dumas muttered.

"And Aimee, I'd like to go through menus for the coming week with you this evening," Rick added.

"Are you planning to sleep in your parents' room in the hotel, Mr. Rick?" Aimee asked.

Rick shook his head quickly. To sleep in his parents room, with all of their memories around him, was asking too much. "Not yet, Aimee," he said. "I think I'll start off in the bungalow I've always had," he said. "I'm more comfortable there."

"Very good, sir," Aimee said.

Rick clapped his hands. "Right, that's enough talking. Let's all get to work. I want this place sparkling clean by morning."

He thought he noticed a lot of sullen faces, but it was always hard to tell what islanders were thinking. Anyway, they filed out silently and all of Rick's orders were carried out. Aimee cooked a delicious meal that evening and became very coy when Rick praised it extravagantly, saying they'd soon be in the Michelin guide if she kept it up. The next few days they all worked nonstop. Rick took Dumas up with him to repair the roof. They both agreed a new roof was needed, but the patch would hold until they had the money, unless, of course, there was another hurricane.

After a couple of weeks of hard work, Rick was feeling despondent. There was so much that needed to be done. The whole place could do with a new whitewash. He thought the decor in the bedrooms looked cheap and he hated the lounge furniture. He knew that the actual building had run into thousands more than his parents had expected, so they had been forced to cut back on the final touches, but guests expected a certain degree of quality from a hotel like this. He sat in the bar and stared out across the almost deserted beach. At this time of year it should be full of umbrellas and lawn chairs. He had done the rounds of all island travel agents, reassuring them that the hotel would remain open, and he'd mailed off brochures to the list of agents his parents had sent to in the States, but other than grabbing people off cruise ships, he didn't know how to get clients. He had been organizing the bar and mentally noting how many supplies needed reordering. He hoped that the life insurance policy came through soon. He hated worrying about money. He was the sort of person who was born to enjoy life, and he hadn't had a second to enjoy it for a long time. He had seriously begun to doubt that he could fulfill his parents' dream after all. He could keep the place clean and attractive and the grounds weeded, but what did he know about marketing and advertising and pleasing guests once they got there? He suspected that it took a lot of money, which he didn't have and didn't seem likely to get.

He looked up in surprise as he heard the light tap of high heels across the marble floor. A woman's voice called out clearly, "Hello, is anybody around?"

Rick leapt out of the bar. He put a hand up to smooth back his hair as he stepped out into the foyer.

"Good afternoon, may I help you?" he asked.

The figure was silhouetted against the light of the front door. Rick noted that it was a very curvy, attractive figure. As she stepped farther into the interior, he saw that she was a good-looking young woman. He judged her to be in her twenties. She was dressed in white shorts that revealed long, athletic legs and a silk shirt with the top three buttons undone. Rick caught a provocative glimpse of breast and admired the young woman's style. Her face was perfectly made up, her pale, sleek hair immaculately in place. Her high-heeled white sandals revealed red-polished toes. Everything about the woman radiated expensive elegance, and Rick thought that she was probably the sort who would be more at home in New York or Miami than in a backwater like this. This was confirmed by the way she looked around with a kind of bored disdain. Immediately Rick was conscious of the tackiness of his furniture—the rattan armchairs and glass-topped tables were hardly what anyone would call elegant. He wanted to apologize for it, to tell her to come back in a few weeks and everything would be just as she desired.

Her gaze settled on Rick. She had interesting dark blue, almost violet eyes . They took in his old white shirt and shorts. "Is this place open?" she demanded.

"Yes, it is," Rick said.

She looked around again. "Is there anybody who can get me a drink?"

"Certainly, what would you like?" Rick asked.

"Are you allowed to serve drinks?" she said. "Isn't there a proper barman?"

"It's his day off," Rick replied.

"Then where's the manager?"

"It's his day off too," Rick said, trying not to smile. The snobby broad was annoying the hell out of him, and it was rather amusing to see that he could annoy her back. "They seem to have left me in charge. I could fix you a drink if you wanted something really simple."

She let out a very pointed sigh. "Oh, all right. I really am thirsty and there's no place else between here and town. I hadn't realized—this island's bigger than you think. I was sightseeing and now I'm just dying of thirst. What do you suggest?"

She sat on one of the rattan stools and crossed her legs provocatively. Again Rick was tempted to tell her there was water in the pump outside, but he remembered that he was supposed to be running a hotel and that he'd often have to deal with difficult guests. "Fresh-squeezed lime juice with rum is very refreshing," he said. "We grow our own limes and Philips's famous rum comes from the island."

"That will do fine," she said with a wave of her hand. Rick noticed the flash of diamonds. He found himself giving the glass an extra polish before he filled it up. The woman acknowledged it with a curt nod of her head, drank it down, then opened her wallet. "How much do I owe you?" she asked.

Rick was tempted to say two dollars, but he said, "Fifty cents, thank you."

She laughed as if this were ridiculously inexpensive and

put two dollar bills down on the table. "I don't suppose you know of anyplace on this side of the island where I can get lunch, do you? I'm suddenly starving. Is there anywhere a little ... uh ... better than this?"

"There's nothing between here and town," Rick said. His anger had been slowly boiling. It seemed as if she was deliberately trying to infuriate him with put-downs.

She sighed again. "Then I suppose this will have to do," she said. "Do you think you could send up the chef, or is it his day off too?"

Rick could stand it no longer. "I'm sorry, ma'am," he said, "but this is a very exclusive hotel. We couldn't possibly serve lunch to just anyone without a reservation. If you'd like to give me your name, maybe we could fit you in sometime next week?"

The young woman's face had gone very red. She got to her feet. "I'll report you to your employer for this," she said.

Rick grinned. "Okay, go ahead. Tell me," he said.

"What do you mean?"

"This is my hotel, and I'm real choosy about who I serve here," he said.

"Then you're a fool," she retorted. "My friends, the Mr. Andrew Vanderbilts, who have that estate on Bell Point, will be arriving next week, and you can be sure I won't be recommending their guests dine here, which is a shame. It might have put your shabby little hotel on the map!"

With that she swept out, her heels angrily tapping down the steps and across the gravel. Rick heard a car engine rev and tires screech as she drove away.

Grace Nobel's face was still hot as she swung the car out onto the road and headed back for her bungalow. How dare he! The rudeness, the stupidity! "Lazy islander," she muttered. What a way to run a hotel. She would never go back there again. And he was completely to blame for letting her think he was a busboy. He had made a fool of her. But as she drove on, a nagging little voice inside her head began to whisper that she was the one who should be ashamed. The more she thought about how she had behaved, the worse she felt. What on earth had made her act that way toward that poor man? Hadn't she always despised those rich women who flung their weight around when she was a humble Pan Am stewardess?

Grace shifted uncomfortably in her seat. She had no idea what had come over her. She didn't usually behave like that to perfect strangers. It wasn't that he was rude to her first. On the contrary, he had been quite friendly until she started having a minor temper tantrum. It must have something to do with the young man, she decided, and the way he looked at her. For most of her life, and especially since she had been able to dress with expensive elegance, men had looked at her with appreciation and frank desire. It was odd that this man hadn't looked at her in that way. He was definitely very good-looking in a boyish sort of way, and she could sense a raw masculinity in his stance. But he had looked as if he saw right through her. I know what you are, his eyes seemed to be saying. You're not what you pretend to be. You're just a nobody who has latched on to a good thing and is making the most of it.

"No!" she said out loud, banging her palm onto the

leather steering wheel of her white convertible. "That's not true."

But was it true? she asked herself. Had she really been kidding herself that she was in love with Andrew Vanderbilt? If he hadn't been so unbelievably rich, would she have looked at him twice? She remembered the first time she had seen him from behind the curtain of the galley in the first class cabin. "That's Andrew Vanderbilt," one of the other stewardesses had whispered. "You know, Vanderbilt steel, Vanderbilt oil?" Grace had peeked. He was an older man, maybe in his forties, his hair graying at the temples, a strong face, very determined jaw. One look at him and you knew that this was a man who got what he wanted.

Grace had seized her chance and gone straight up to him. "Good afternoon, Mr. Vanderbilt, welcome aboard. Is there anything I can get you while we wait for takeoff?" she asked.

A smile spread across his face while he took her in. "Now, how did you know my name?" he asked.

"Weren't you on the cover of *Time*?" she asked. "Some oil deal in the Middle East? I know I've recently read about you. Of course, you were Man of the Year!"

He looked impressed. "A well-read young woman," he said. "Now, would an educated young woman like yourself know how to make a perfectly dry martini, one that merely glimpses the vermouth bottle?"

"And has a twist of lemon but no olive?" she retorted.

His smile spread. "Exactly," he commented.

When they disembarked in Paris he invited her to dine with him at the Ritz that evening. Over dinner she found out just how lucky she had been. He had taken a commercial flight only because his private plane had gone in for emergency repairs. The next day a bracelet of perfect Cartier pearls arrived at Grace's hotel. The next night she spent with Andrew at his apartment overlooking the Bois de Boulogne. She had to leave the morning after that, but Andrew miraculously showed up on the next legs of her run in Athens and Beirut, and within a month his private jet was flying her to meet him at his various houses around the world.

At first it was like a fantasy: private jets, expensive presents, dinner at the best restaurants in the world. She kept pinching herself and reminding herself that it couldn't last. But then one day, as they sat overlooking the Seine, he had said in his businesslike way, "I've come to a decision. I've decided I'm a little too old for this."

"Too old for what?" she had asked, terrified that he was finding a polite way to break up with her.

"Too old to go chasing you around the world," he said. "It's upsetting my schedule to have to keep pace with yours, which leaves me only one alternative."

Grace held her breath and waited for the worst.

"You have to quit that damn job of yours," he said. "I know you love flying, but I sort of hoped that you love me more. You could travel with me when I go to meetings—pretend you're some sort of very private secretary if you like."

Grace laughed with relief and joy. "Okay," she said, "but is it usual to take dictation at night?"

"When you're Andrew Vanderbilt, you can give dictation whenever you damn well please," he said, laughing at her excited face. "You do love me, don't you, Gracie?"

"You know I do," she said, and she realized that it was true. It wasn't just the trappings she liked, although they were wonderful. She liked being with him. She liked his strength and his power, the fast pace of his life. She liked his lovemaking too. There had been a few men in her life before, but she had gotten tired of them all rather quickly. To Andrew, lovemaking was an art to be savored, not rushed. He played her body like an exquisite instrument. He had a thousand different ways of touching and arousing her, making her feel as if her body were a burning volcano about to explode. When he finally entered her, she found herself crying out with desire.

Thinking of him now made Grace ache with desire. It had been more than two weeks since they had been together. She couldn't wait for his arrival the following day. She just prayed that this arrangement would work, that he'd really manage to get away from his family and be with her. His family, of course, was the fly in Grace's ointment, the only thing that spoiled this otherwise perfect relationship. Andrew had a wife and two children, whom he adored. He admitted that he didn't love his wife, but he was not going to do anything that would make life complicated for his children. His wife had made it clear that she wouldn't give him a divorce under any circumstances, even though she was scarcely more interested in him than he was in her, and Andrew was adamant that he was not going to subject his children to an explosive legal battle.

A few weeks earlier he had told Grace that he usually spent a great deal of the winter with his family at their

Caribbean retreat. "You'd like St. Martin, he said to Grace. "It's half French, half Dutch: a pleasant little island, not at all touristy. Great beaches, good rum."

Grace smiled ruefully. "I doubt whether I'm ever going to see it," she said. "I don't expect I'd be welcome at your family's home."

"Which is why I've just entered into a little real estate deal," Andrew said, his eyes lighting up as they always did when he had a surprise for her. "I've purchased a little cottage. It's really quite pretty—wonderful cliff-top view of the best beach on the island, called Baie Rouge. I think you'll like it."

Grace's eyes opened wide. "You bought it for me?"

Andrew ran his fingers along her thigh. "My dear, you don't think I could be without you for four whole weeks, do you?" he said.

"But won't your wife be suspicious if you keep popping out to see me?"

His face grew cold. "My wife usually retires to bed around nine with an inch of cream on her face and two sleeping pills," he said. "And I am in the habit of going for late-night walks along the beach." He gave her a long, satisfied smile.

Thinking of that smile now and the way Andrew looked at her produced the same dull ache in the pit of her belly. God, how she wanted him, how she longed for him! She didn't care if he was married. She knew he really belonged to her, and when he came to her little cliff-top cottage, he'd forget any other woman ever existed!

She swung the car off the road, past a riotous bougainvillea hedge, and into her driveway. Tomorrow

Andrew would be here and everything would be just perfect again. And if she ever bumped into that attractive guy from the hotel, she'd just have to make her peace with him and be very nice …. maybe she and Andrew might even go over there for a meal ….

CHAPTER 4

From her cliff-top garden Grace watched the Learjet make its approach, then dip behind the mountain to land on the other side of the island. It had to be Andrew's plane, she told herself. She wondered if he'd call her from the airport. Grace instantly reminded herself that there would hardly be an opportunity if his family was there to meet him.

In the past Grace had tried not to be curious about Andrew's family. She reasoned that they were one part of his life and she was another. Her meetings with Andrew had usually been far from where his family was living. There was never any reason to think or worry about them. But now that they were on the same small island, her curiosity was piqued. She wanted to see for herself these other people who had a claim to Andrew's affection.

At first she found herself looking into expensive cars as they drove past, staring at women shopping in the exclusive boutiques, and sitting near children playing on the beaches, wondering if any of them could be Andrew's family. Finally the temptation became too great. She drove up to the Bell Point compound and parked in a shady spot off the road. She hadn't been there long when the gates opened and a white Mercedes convertible swept out, catching Grace by surprise. All she saw was an impression of a long, aristocratic sort of face, long red nails on the steering wheel, and a beige silk scarf tied over ash-brown curls. In the seat beside her a young girl kneeled backward, looking out. Grace clearly saw a child, a little girl who looked much like Andrew when he was thinking hard. The little girl had spotted her car and peered out with definite interest as the Mercedes swung around a corner and vanished around the bend.

Grace drove home feeling shaken and thoughtful. His wife Catherine posed no threat to her: She was cold and spoiled and Grace knew from Andrew that she was more interested in her racehorses than she was in people. But thinking of that little girl, Grace was overcome with chills. How could she ever compete for Andrew's affection with so lovely a child? It suddenly hit Grace that she'd never be more than an accessory in Andrew's life. His favorite accessory, maybe, but never anything more.

Her insecurity continued to nag at her all week. Even after she saw his plane, Grace convinced herself that it might be days before he'd have a chance to visit her. Just in case, she fixed her hair and nails and put on a white lace sundress that Andrew particularly liked.

At nine o'clock she chided herself for being stupid. Of course he wasn't coming. There would be dinner with the family, playing with the children, and visiting with a wife he hadn't seen in a couple of months. Grace decided to hell with everything. It was a hot, sticky evening and she was going for a swim. She stepped out of her dress and into her bikini, then, draping a towel around her shoulders, ran down the flight of steps to her little private beach below. Lights twinkled in the calm water from her cottage on the cliff top. The dark water felt refreshingly cool, and she stood for a moment, thigh-deep, letting the gentle waves nudge past her before she dove in and started swimming.

Grace had always prided herself on her swimming. She had been one of the most athletic girls at school and had won many ribbons and trophies for swimming and other sports. Although she had been out of school for several years now, she kept her body in tiptop shape. She was proud of her firm breasts, muscular thighs, and flat stomach. She moved through the black waters in an effortless crawl, delighting in the power of her stroke and the feeling of cool water rushing past her body. When she was far from shore she lay on her back, looking up at the canopy of stars, letting all the tensions of the day slip away from her.

When something brushed against her leg she reacted quickly, realizing that she was quite a way from shore and that sharks were always a possibility in these warm waters. She struck out for shore. Swimming as fast as she could, her panic made it hard to breathe and her arms harder to move. After what seemed like an eternity, she heard the comforting hiss of waves breaking on sand, and her feet touched bottom. As she stood up, her pulse still racing, she saw a figure standing a few feet away. She was about to cry out when she saw that it was Andrew.

He was dressed in a polo shirt and khaki shorts. His gray hair was windswept from driving in an open car, and he looked even more handsome than she remembered.

"No," he said, eyeing her with obvious pleasure. "It's not a mermaid. Pity. I've always wanted to meet one."

He walked into the water to meet her as she came toward him.

"Mermaids have tails," she said. Her delight in seeing him had banished all other emotions. "And they don't usually wear bikinis."

"Easily remedied," he said. Deftly he reached around behind her and flicked open the catch on her bikini. As it fell, his hands came around her breasts, his fingers warm against her cold, wet flesh. She gave a little sigh of desire. "I've missed you," he said, drawing her toward him. He kissed her hard on the mouth. "You taste of salt, " he said, laughing, "and my doctor's just put me on a low-salt diet."

"Aren't you allowed to break your diet now and then?" she whispered, her eyes teasing him.

"For you, anything," he murmured, his voice thick with passion. He began to unbutton his shirt and shorts.

"Shouldn't we go up to the house?" she asked, looking around uneasily.

"I can't wait that long," he said. "Besides, I've never made love in the ocean."

"But anyone could see us."

He laughed and kicked off his shorts impatiently. As he moved toward her, he whispered, "If they're watching, they might learn a thing or two."

He kissed her again, her chilled body delighting in the rough warmth of his chest against her. His hands traveled down her as they sank into the soft white sand. Grace was excited, ready for him, wanting him as much as he wanted her. He kissed her deeply, sensing her urgency. His tongue explored the inside of her mouth. He bit her lip as they began making love with a passion that made her cry out. Waves came rushing up, hissing over the sand and splashing over them, intensifying their fire. It was over too soon for both of them. They were gasping as they lay still, water dripping from their hair, gently rocking with the incoming tide.

Andrew moved away from her with regret. "I think we're in danger of being swept out to sea," he said.

She smiled at him tenderly. "What a lovely way to die," she said. "Locked in each other's arms until we sink beneath the waves."

"You're a hopeless romantic," he said, taking her hand to pull her to her feet. "I do not intend to go gently, embraced or otherwise. Come on, you're shivering. Let's go back to the cottage."

He held out his shirt for her to cover up, then wrapped the towel around his waist. "Come on, my mermaid," he said. "I wonder if it would be more interesting with a tail …."

"Meaning I don't excite you enough the way I am?" She demanded. "That was just the appetizer we had down there. Wait until I get you up to the cottage for the main course." She brushed seductively against him, then ran past him to the steps. "Come on, old guy. See if you can catch me!" she called, then sprang up the steep steps like a young gazelle.

Andrew watched her long legs in admiration, then snatched up his clothes and ran after her. They arrived panting and laughing at the top of the steps. "You'll be the death of me, young Grace," he said, his breath coming in great gulps. "I'm going to have to take a breather before any thought of the next course."

"Nonsense. You're fitter than I am, and you know it," she said. "You'll still be doing this when you're ninety-nine." As she said it, she felt a deep stab of regret. Andrew might still be doing it, but it wouldn't be with her. It would be with a younger, more desirable body than hers, whom his money could still afford to buy.

The cottage felt warm and welcoming after the chill of the night breeze on their wet skin. Grace went into the bedroom and came out with a sheer robe loosely wrapped around her.

"I'll fix us both a drink," she said. "Rum punch or your favorite martini?"

"When on the island, we'd better live like islanders," he said. "Make it a rum punch."

She poured a generous splash of rum into two tall glasses, then added ice, a dash of curaçao, grenadine, lime juice, and lots of fresh fruit. Andrew drank his down. "I must say, that refreshes," he said. "Now I feel ready for anything."

"Oh, what did you have in mind?" Grace asked, lowering herself onto his knee.

"You're an insatiable young woman," he said, slapping her thigh playfully. "Wait one minute. I've brought you something." He eased her off his knee and moved the table. A long red leather box lay there. He brought it over to her. "Here," he said. "A belated Christmas present."

"Oh, Andrew," she said, her eyes opening wide with anticipation. She'd never even seen a box like this. The red leather had faded with age, but it was still very rich-looking and embossed with gold. "What a beautiful box," she exclaimed, running her fingers over the surface.

"Go on, open it," Andrew said impatiently.

She flicked open the catch and gasped as lamplight glittered on diamonds and rubies. It was a priceless set of jewelry: There was a bracelet of matched rubies and diamonds, an elegant ruby ring, teardrop earrings ... but the pièce de résistance was the necklace. It was the sort of necklace she'd seen only in museums and maybe Tiffany's window. At its center was a ruby pendant which must have been seven or eight carats.

"Andrew" was all she could say. Never in her life could she have dreamed of owning anything like this. "It's the crown jewels," she said, realizing how idiotic and girlish she must sound.

He laughed and looked pleased. "You're right," he said. "It once belonged to an empress."

"You're kidding."

"Scout's honor," he said, laughing at her face. "This once graced the ample bosom of Empress Marie Feodorovna of Russia, so the experts at Sotheby's tell me."

"I can't believe it," she said, taking the necklace from the box and letting the stones spill through her fingers like liquid fire. "Help me put it on."

She turned away while he clasped it at her neck. As she turned back to him, she let her robe fall away. She stood there in front of him, naked except for the necklace, and began to model it for him. As she walked past him, her breasts swayed provocatively beneath the rubies. "Does it suit me?" she whispered. She went over to the mirror and stared at herself, marveling at the exquisite stones.

"I think it suits you much better than it did old Empress Marie." Andrew came up behind her, sliding his hands around to cup her breasts, and leaned over to kiss her neck.

"I think I'm ready for the main course after all," he whispered, then swept her up into his arms and carried her over to the bed. Grace could feel the gems digging into her skin as his body pressed against hers. "Oh, yes, Andrew, yes!" she called out, arching her back as his hands moved slowly down her body in one fluid caress. He buried his face in her throat as they came together in unbridled passion. She heard him cry out. Suddenly he seemed to gasp for air. He rolled away from her, clutching at his chest. He shook convulsively, and then nothing. He lay perfectly still.

"Andrew?" she screamed. "What is it? What's the matter?"

He lay unmoving. His face was ashen. She slapped his cheeks and grabbed his wrist, feeling for a pulse. There was none. "No," she screamed, overwhelmed with helplessness. As an airline hostess, she had been trained in first aid. She began to administer CPR, pounding futilely on his chest. After several minutes had passed, she gave up. She had to admit that his heart was not going to start beating again. There was an ambulance in the hospital over on the Dutch side, but it was almost an hour away, which would be too late.

As she emerged from a fog of despair, the situation became clear to her. There would be scandal, international publicity ... she'd be in the tabloids, as would his family. Grace made her decision quickly. Andrew would have wanted to protect his children at any cost. She would try to carry out his wishes. There would be no police, no ambulance. She'd make it look as if he had gone for a late-night walk on his own grounds and had succumbed to a heart attack.

It wasn't easy. She was shaking so violently, her teeth wouldn't stop chattering. As she dressed herself and found his clothes, she kept glancing at his body, praying that she'd been wrong and he would wake up again. She half expected to find him looking at her quizzically. "What are you looking like that for?" he'd demand. "What's the fuss about?"

But his body already felt cold as she dressed him in his shorts and shirt. It was like dressing a mannequin. His car was waiting in the driveway outside—the Land Rover he used to get around the island. She drove it up to the front door and then began the laborious process of dragging his body out to the car. She was sweating and trembling all over by the time she lowered him into the passenger seat. Before leaving she went back into the house for a shot of rum to steady her.

Grace drove as far as the gates of Bell Point, using Andrew's automatic opener to make the tall wrought iron gates swing open noiselessly. She turned off the lights and cut the engine, letting the car coast down the gentle slope, until it stopped about a hundred yards from the house. This would be a logical place to park if he'd decided to take a walk down to the beach. He'd come up again and the steps had been too much for him.

She realized with a jolt what she was saying to herself: She had made him run up all those steps, teased him into making love with her again. If his doctor had just put him on a low-salt diet, it must have been because he had high blood pressure or a weak heart. Grace felt clammy with guilt and horror. To know that Andrew had died was bad enough. To know that she might have caused his death was unbearable. All she wanted to do was to end this mission and get back to the safety of her little cottage.

Using every ounce of her strength, she dragged him from the car until he collapsed in a heap on the grass. At least his fall looked natural. Nobody should ever suspect. She left the keys in the car and started to creep away. As she reached the gates she looked back at the house. A light was shining in an upstairs window. The curtain was pulled back and a small face looked out. It was too distant for Grace to make out who it was, but she shrank back into the cover of the bushes and sprinted for the gate only after the curtain fell again. She ran the entire three miles back to the cottage and crawled into bed with her clothes on. After an hour or so her crying gave way and Grace fell into a deep sleep.

The next day the news made headlines in all the island papers. The overseas edition of the *New York Times* announced that oil magnate and tycoon Andrew Vanderbilt had died of a heart attack at his Caribbean retreat. On the St. Martin French radio station the same news was announced, followed by the information that Mr. Vanderbilt was to be cremated in a private ceremony on Thursday and his ashes shipped back to be scattered into Long Island Sound, beside his beloved New York mansion. Grace thought privately that he'd probably prefer his ashes to be scattered here in the warm Caribbean. Then she decided that Andrew would think it was all a "waste of time and energy." She could almost hear him saying the words, and she smiled for the first time since his death.

She drove down to the airport after the funeral had taken place and watched Andrew's widow and children board his private plane. Andrew's widow looked impressive, dressed in black with a smart black hat on her head and a little veil covering her face. The two children were also dressed in black —the boy a gawky twelve-year-old looking rather ridiculous in short pants, and the little girl in a stiff dress that was too big for her. As they climbed the steps to the plane, Sophie paused and looked back. It seemed to Grace that she sought her out among the crowd of curious locals and stared straight at her. The gaze was so fierce and penetrating that it made Grace wanted to run away. Then the child was called from inside the plane, and she disappeared. But Grace was now sure that hers had been the face looking out of the upstairs window and that she knew, beyond any shadow of a doubt, who Grace was and what had happened that night.

The next week the headline read VANDERBILT CHILDREN INHERIT HALF A BILLION. The article went on to say that apart from generous bequests to his various charitable foundations, Andrew's entire estate was to be divided in trust between his two children, Jack and Sophie. Until now money had been the last thing on Grace's mind, but she was shocked as she read the article. Andrew had told her more than once that she'd never have to worry about money again. He told her that he was willing a generous amount to her so she'd be well taken care of if anything happened to him. She didn't quite know how to go about finding out the details, so she drove over to the Dutch side of the island and went to see Van Pelt, the young lawyer who had handled her real estate transaction. He promised he'd look into things for her. When he called her back a few days later, the news was not good.

"I'm sorry to tell you this," he said. "The information reported in the paper was essentially true."

"You mean Andrew left me nothing?"

"The deed to the cottage is in your name," he said, clearing his throat awkwardly. "I'm very sorry, Miss Nobel."

"Don't be," she said. "It's not as if I were old or helpless. I'm young. I've worked for my living before and I can do so again."

"Do you want me to sell the cottage for you?" he asked. "The market's really booming right now. I could get you a good price."

"No, thank you," she said. "I'll never sell the cottage. It's all I have to remind me of Andrew. I'll hang on to it whatever happens."

Grace took a deep breath as she replaced the phone on its receiver. She had several pieces of good jewelry, one fabulous set of rubies and diamonds, an island cottage, but virtually no money. Thinking clearly, she took stock. As she gazed out of her window, smelling the salty air and looking at the riot of greenery and the sparkling ocean beyond, she realized that she never wanted to go back to the life she had before—dodging taxis, snow and slush, pushing through mad crowds. She had already slowed to the island pace and she wanted to stay put. She had no idea what she would use for money or what she would do with herself, but she knew she was not going back to the States again!

CHAPTER 5

Robert Philips was never sure that he liked New York. Perhaps, in theory, it sounded wonderful. In fact, it lured and beckoned to him when he was studying in the austere quiet of his room in New Haven. At Yale he sometimes felt hemmed in by the four walls and stifled by the weight of academia around him. Then New York seemed an exciting mecca of dazzle and excitement.

"Maybe I'll go into town for a day, see a show, take in a nightclub," Robert would say to himself, knowing guiltily that he should be finishing a paper. But once he got there, the city quickly overwhelmed him. So many flashing lights, so much dirt and squalor, so many people. It was so fast-paced, so big, so impersonal. If you hesitated at the curb for a second after the lights changed, you were pushed off. If you stepped out to cross on the green when a taxi wanted to make a turn, you were sworn at. New York made Robert realize that, for all his American education, he was an islander and he could never face a long-term future in the States.

It was about a month before finals and Robert, feeling another bout of academic claustrophobia coming on, came up to New York for the day. The weather had been depressingly cold and gray. It seemed that spring would never arrive in New Haven. As he watched rain drip from bare tree branches, his whole being longed for the brightness and warmth of the Caribbean. The paper he was attempting to write seemed completely uninspired and pedantic. He needed inspiration and he needed it fast.

As he stepped out of Grand Central Station into the crowds, he felt the usual rush of excitement. He spent a pleasant morning divided between Bloomingdale's and the Metropolitan Museum of Art. For lunch he grabbed a Coney Island dog from a corner street vendor and felt sick after it. The usual New York panic began to set in: millions of people hurrying by to their own destinations and he didn't know one of them. There was not one person in this whole city who knew his name! Back home, everyone knew the Philipses. Although the weather was getting worse, sending great gusts of wind racing up from the East River, he decided that a walk around Central Park would do him good. He felt starved for color: Every New Yorker seemed to be dressed in black, the buildings were gray, the sky was gray, even the air seemed heavy with gray filth. Last time he had been there, the earliest spring flowers had been about to come up in Central Park. Maybe a bed of yellow daffodils would lift his spirits.

He started up Fifth Avenue, glancing in the expensive store windows and smiling at the ridiculous prices. At home he was used to feeling rich but he had never, in his wildest dreams, wanted to pay fifty dollars for a tie or a belt—especially when that tie and belt looked very much like the things he had just seen for ten dollars in Bloomingdales. New Yorkers must be stupid, Robert decided. He was glad he didn't have to live here ....

It was then that he saw the young woman. In a city of no color she stood out like a flaming beacon. The first thing he noticed about her was her hair. She had a magnificent mane of flame-red hair that tumbled down her back and contrasted brilliantly with the emerald-green coat she was wearing. The second thing he noticed was that the coat looked as if it covered a very shapely figure. The third thing Robert became aware of was how she stared into Tiffany's window. There was such a faraway longing in her eyes that Robert was immediately touched. Nothing in Tiffany's could compete with her own beauty, he thought. What could she possibly want? If he had any money to speak of in his pocket, he would have run inside and bought her something.

Robert was not the sort of person who picked up strange women, especially not in the middle of New York City. But he had never found anyone so irresistibly attractive before. No other woman had struck him with that combination of innocence and sensuality. He stood there, watching her, telling himself that he should walk on, yet he was unable to do so. At last he could stand it no longer. He stepped up beside her and pretended to look at the jewels. When he heard her give a little sigh, he took it as his cue.

"They're very beautiful, aren't they?" he said in his smooth, deep voice.

She looked up at him, her eyes shining. "Yes, they are," she said. "It makes me feel good just to look at them."

Her eyes were fabulous—cat's eyes with a greenish tint — and he found himself bewitched by them. "Do you live around here?" he asked boldly.

The young woman laughed. "Oh, no. I just come up this way shopping sometimes. I shouldn't be here at all, in fact ... what time is it?"

Robert glanced at his watch. "Twenty past two."

The sparkle immediately left her eyes. "Oh, no. I must be getting back," she said. "I've stayed out too long."

She started to move away. "Wait," he called, running to catch up with her. He had a sudden inspiration. "Look, I have an appointment in a few minutes. Can I give you a ride?"

She gave an incredulous smile. "But you don't even know where I'm going. It might be completely in the opposite direction."

"I'm not in that much of a hurry. I can drop you off somewhere, unless it's Staten Island or Hoboken."

"It's back on Twenty-third street," she said.

"Then that's perfect," Robert lied. "My appointment is down on Wall Street."

"In that case," the woman said, and gave him a wonderful smile.

Robert hailed a taxi. Miraculously it stopped for him. He felt excited and powerful as he opened the door and helped her in.

They sat in awkward silence. He was conscious of her closeness. She smelled faintly of perfume and one of her long, shapely legs brushed against his pants.

"Horrible weather, isn't it?" Robert said at last. "I'm

beginning to think spring will never come."

She nodded. He noticed that the wistful look was beginning to come back into her eyes. At last she said, "Look ... uh ... sir, I think I should tell you that I'm a married woman. My husband gets angry if I'm out too long. That's why I really appreciate this ride back. I didn't mean to walk all the way up Fifth Avenue. I just lost track of the time."

Robert, fighting his overwhelming disappointment, managed to be a true gentleman.

"I'm glad I could be of help."

She turned those appealing eyes on him again. "Oh, you have been," she said. "You saved my life."

She said this as if it were really true, and not just a figure of speech.

For once the taxi hit every green light and Twenty-third Street came up far too quickly.

"What number?" Robert asked.

"The west three hundred block. You can pull right up in front of the Orchid Dry Cleaners," she said, "but you don't have to...."

"It's no trouble," Robert said. He wanted her beside him as long as possible.

The taxi swung to the right along twenty-third and pulled up outside the dry cleaners.

"I have to drop my husband's suits off," she said, pointing to the bag she was carrying. "He likes them just so. He's very fussy about the way he looks."

Robert got out and opened the door for her. He held out his hand to steady her down to the sidewalk, and she took it. For a second her hand was warm in his. It seemed to Robert that she lingered a little longer than she needed to before she skipped lightly onto the sidewalk and turned to give him another dazzling smile.

"I really can't thank you enough," she said. "I enjoyed meeting you."

Robert wanted to ask her name and tell her his, but traffic had already begun to build behind the waiting taxi and the street was filled with impatient drivers. The woman looked back at him once more, a sort of wistful smile this time, then darted into the store. Reluctantly Robert got into his taxi and went on his way.

Through the years Robert had had his share of girlfriends. He had even been in love a couple of times, but he had never felt like this about a woman before. He went to see a Broadway play and all he could see was her face. He thought about her on his train ride home. He lay awake, staring at his ceiling, thinking about her. He wanted her so badly, he really believed that if he didn't get her, he would die. He reasoned with himself that she was a married woman. For her, this had just been a pleasant encounter to be forgotten the moment she got home, but he couldn't believe that. He had seen unhappiness in those gorgeous cat-eyes, and he had seen them light up when she looked at him. She was definitely interested, he told himself.

The next morning he got up early and caught a commuter train to New York. It was a miserable day. The wind off the river cut right through him. He drank cup after cup of bad coffee in a little café across the street from the cleaners. Through the café window he could keep an eye on the entrance. But she didn't come out. When the cleaners closed at six, he had to admit defeat and caught the train back home.

He was up most of the night working on the paper he had neglected, but the next morning he caught the same early train back to the city. Her husband must surely need those suits by now. She'd have to come back for them today. Then a depressing thought struck him. What if her husband had been in yesterday to pick them up for himself?

"You're acting like a fool," he told himself. Usually he was known as the sensible one in the family. When Will had climbed down the cliff and had to be rescued, Robert sat at the top and didn't go with him. Will used to spend all his allowance at once and eat all his Easter candy in one day. Robert would save his pennies and make his Easter candy last for a month. Christof, Will, and Rick used to tease him about it.

"This one was born grown-up," Christof used to say.

Now he was acting like a lovesick boy. He knew he was being stupid, but he couldn't stop himself. He knew that his graduation would be jeopardized if he didn't turn in the paper, but he caught the train to New York the next day.

She never came and Robert got very wet standing out in a steady downpour. By the third day he was beginning to believe he had lost her. He was doing all this for nothing. Someone else had picked up the cleaning and he'd never see her again. His rational side said to forget her and get on with his life, but his romantic side whispered that she had been interested in him. If he waited long enough, she'd have to return.

On the third day he was rewarded: He looked across the street, and there, behind a black umbrella, he saw a mass of red curls. His heart started racing. He was finding it hard to breathe as she approached the dry cleaners. He crossed the street and approached her as she opened the door.

"Well, hi there," he said, tapping her shoulder. He tried to sound casually surprised. He had practiced it a thousand times in his head and it came out pretty well. "Are you in need of another taxi?"

Letting the door bang shut, she turned and looked at him suspiciously. Then her face lit up.

"Hello," she said. "What are you doing here?"

"Oh, just some business in the neighborhood," he said. "It's amazing, isn't it? All these people in New York and I happen to run into you twice in a week."

"Amazing," she said.

"Look, I was just about to go have lunch," he said, quickly checking his watch to find out what time of day it was. "I don't suppose you have time to join me? I hate eating alone."

She looked around, worried and confused. "Oh, no. I really should be … I mean, it wouldn't be wise …."

"I'm not asking you to run away with me to Las Vegas," he said. "Just a perfectly civilized lunch in a coffee shop."

Her eyes lit up. Robert had dreamed about them for three nights now, but he had forgotten the power of that smile. "Why not?" she said. "I won't be missed for another hour. But let's go over to the next block. I know of a nicer café."

He wanted to take her arm as they walked together. He wanted to take her hand and run with her down the sidewalk, swept along by the powerful wind, but he managed to make small talk until they were safely seated in The Garden Spot. They were offered a table in the window, but she shook her head quickly.

"Back there would be nicer," she said, and hurried to a little table in a corner. Robert sat opposite her. He watched, fascinated, as she unbuttoned her overcoat and let it slide off. Underneath she was wearing a thin white silky sweater with a low scooped neck that revealed the promise of a magnificent pair of breasts. He thought that these were rounder and smoother and more shapely than any breasts he had ever seen. He could even make out the shape of her nipples through the sweater, and he felt his pulse race. He knew he was grinning like a little boy with a new toy, but he couldn't help it.

"I do believe," she said slowly, "that you didn't bump into me by accident at all. I believe you engineered this. Am I right?"

He looked down, annoyed that he was blushing. "A little, maybe," he said. "I couldn't stop thinking about you."

"There's no point in thinking about me," she said flatly. "I'm married. In fact, you mustn't think about me. It wouldn't be wise. My husband is not an easy man. He gets upset quickly."

As she looked away, he thought that her right eye seemed hollow and darker than the left. It was cleverly disguised with makeup, but he was pretty sure that she had the remains of a black eye. His senses were roused. He wanted to find the guy right now and knock him to the ground. Beat him to a pulp.

"I don't even know your name," he said. "I've thought about you for three whole days and I haven't had a name to put to your face."

"It's Laetitia," she said. "Laetitia Gambetti." She pronounced it in the Italian way.

"Oh, I see," he said. "A real Italian *contessa*."

She laughed. "Hardly a *contessa*."

"You look like one to me," he said. "I'm Robert, by the way. Robert Philips."

"And you live in New York, Mr. Philips?"

"Call me Robert, for heaven's sake," he said. "No, I live in New Haven right now. I'm a student at Yale."

"Then all that stuff about business appointments on Wall Street ...?" she said quickly.

"I might be the sort of Yale student who dabbles in the stock market in his spare time," he said.

"But you're not?"

He shook his head.

"I'm flattered that you'd go to all this trouble for me," she said.

"You're not the sort of person one meets often in life," he said. "I couldn't let you slip away from me."

She reached out a hand and covered his. "Look, Mr .... Robert. Don't talk that way. I can't see you again. I keep telling you I'm married."

"Happily married?"

"That's not the point," she said. "I'm Italian. We take our marriage vows very seriously. The church doesn't believe in divorce and neither does my husband. He'd rather have me dead than with another man."

"He treats you badly?"

She looked away. "Let's just say that life with him is not exactly easy. He has a very quick temper and he likes everything just right. He gets annoyed when Joey makes a mess or cries."

"Joey?"

She raised her eyes to meet his. "That's another reason I can't leave. I have a little boy. Three years old. He's the one thing I live for."

"Why on earth did you marry this man if he's such a brute," Robert blurted out, realizing as he asked that the question wasn't entirely tactful.

But she didn't take offense. She smiled. "He was awfully handsome and he treated me nicely when I first met him. I was eighteen and it was at a cousin's wedding. You know Italian weddings—dancing, feasting, millions of people all related to each other. I saw him across the room and he smiled at me. We danced. He was a great dancer. What did I know about men? He was the cousin of a cousin and my parents seemed to like him. I was sharing a room with two sisters, so I was eager to have my own place. It was only afterward that I found out what he really did for a living …."

"Which is?"

"He works for the Mancini family."

"Doing what?"

Laetitia actually laughed. "They're one of the biggest Mafia families in the country," she said.

"Your husband's in the Mafia?" Robert exclaimed louder than he had intended.

She looked around the room anxiously. "Please, keep

your voice down. It's not something you shout about if you want to stay alive. He's only a small player in the Mancini gang. But yes, that's essentially what he does, and I hate it."

"Aren't you in danger yourself?"

"Probably," she said. "He gets very angry if I ever say anything. I hate it all." She started as a waiter dropped silverware behind her. "Sometimes I feel like a prisoner," she said. "He's at home most of the day and always wants to know where I've been. I take Joey over to my mother's a lot. She makes a big fuss over him and it's safer for him to play there. That's where he is now. I must pick him up in a little while, before Joseph wakes from his nap."

"I don't know what to say," Robert whispered. "You can't go on living like that. We must do something."

She smiled. "You've only just met me. You know nothing about me at all. For all you know, I might be making this up. I might be a typist with a vivid imagination …."

"I know you're not," he said. "The moment I first saw you I knew there was something special about you. I've never felt this way about anybody before, Laetitia, my lovely *contessa*." He paused. "You know your name doesn't suit you at all."

This made her laugh. "I can't help it. That's what I was baptized."

He was looking at her with longing. "I'm going to call you Contessa," he said. "That suits you much better."

"You can call me what you like since we won't be seeing each other again," she said.

"We have to see each other again."

She shook her head firmly. "It's too dangerous," she said.

"Can you understand what my husband and his friends would do to a nice college boy from Yale if they found out he'd been hanging around with his wife? They have their own set of rules, you know. I don't want you to wind up at the bottom of the Hudson River."

"I can't help it, Contessa. I know only that I have to see you again. We'll be very careful. We'll take no chances. Tell me when you take Joey to your mother's. We'll meet here. Nobody would recognize you in a place like this."

She looked around again. "I guess that's true," she said. "It's just that ... you don't know what he's like. He's so frightening when he's angry."

"Then I must find a way to help you get free," he said. "I mean it, Contessa. I really plan to set you free."

He reached out across the table and took her hand. She didn't resist and they sat there, gazing at each other, lost in thoughts of their future together.

CHAPTER 6

W ill Phillips yawned loudly. The professor looked up in annoyance from his lecture, and several students giggled. Will didn't even have the grace to blush. He had no interest at all in the history of sheep farming in America, but he needed one animal husbandry course for his degree at the University of Virginia. In two more months he'd be out of there for good. There was so much he wanted to do, so many places he wanted to see. He wanted to explore the whole world, climb mountains, raft rivers, trek through jungles. Life was full of exciting adventures ... and then there was Marigot ....

His pulse quickened at the thought of her. Meeting her again after so many years was still like a miracle to Will. She was so lovely, so desirable and the most amazing thing was that she found him as attractive as he found her. Will was used to girls hanging around him. All athletes got their share of adoring fans and the pick of the girls in school, but no girl had meant anything before Marigot. He looked around the classroom at the blond ponytails. How juvenile they seemed to him now, how pale and uninteresting, totally girlish and lacking in sex appeal. Marigot was no older than them, and yet she was already a woman in every sense of the word. The thought of her slim brown body sent the blood rushing through his veins. How would he survive for two whole months before he was with her again?

Their time together had been so brief —a stolen embrace in the shadows after the funeral banquet, a few blissful moments together in the boat, and then that one incredible evening, the night before he left. He had been tied up with his father and brother all day, sorting through his mother's things, deciding what to keep and what to give away. It had been a solemn and painful occasion for both Christof and Robert. Will knew he should be feeling grief too, but his mother's death hadn't even sunk in yet. His thoughts kept straying back to Marigot. He wanted her so desperately!

He had an early flight in the morning and he hoped that Marigot would come to say good-bye. He hadn't told anyone what he was feeling about her: He wasn't sure what his father would say, but he knew his brother Robert wouldn't approve. Robert was such a stuffed shirt. He'd always been a stuffed shirt, Will reflected, always warning him not to do crazy things or he'd get into trouble. Robert seemed to have inherited a superiority complex. Natives were great for cutting sugarcane or working in the factory, but you didn't socialize with them. Will remembered now that Robert had even disapproved when he and Marigot used to wrestle as kids.

If only I'd known then, he thought. To have been so close to her, to have pinned her to the ground and thought only of winning the wrestling match. What a waste of opportunity. He knew very well what he would do now if he had her pinned to the ground beneath him.

Evening came, and Will went to pack his bags for the trip back to Virginia, and still she hadn't shown up. Madame de Gaulle supervised dinner as she always did. Will kept glancing nervously at her face to see if she knew about him and Marigot, but Madame de Gaulle's face never gave anything away. As she brought in the fruit bowl and cheese board at the end of the meal he remarked, cleverly he thought, "I should have thought you'd make Marigot do some of this work for you, now that she's home with nothing better to do."

As usual, Madame de Gaulle's face was impassive. "You know Marigot," she said. "You try making her to do anything she doesn't want." Then she swept out of the room. What did she mean by that, Will wondered. She had said, "You know Marigot." Was she hinting that she had seen him with her daughter, kissing in the darkness?

Will got up from the table. "I don't think I'll wait for dessert tonight," he said. "I think I'll go for a stroll if you two will excuse me."

He tried to make an unhurried exit, then ran across the compound to Madame de Gaulle's house. He knew she always stayed around to supervise the cleaning of the kitchen after dinner, which would give him a while yet to find Marigot. As he headed up the little path between the hedges, he hesitated. He had never actually been inside Madame de Gaulle's house. He knew that she demanded her privacy and had insisted on living in her own old-style Caribbean house right on the other side of the property when she came to work for the Philipses. When Robert and Will were young they had speculated a lot about why she chose to live such a private existence. At one stage they decided she might be carrying on voodoo in secret—there always had been something uncanny about the way she knew things, like who had raided the cookie jar. He and Robert had spied on her a few times in his childhood, but had never seen any of the sights they had hoped for. No white roosters had been sacrificed, no one had been turned into a zombie, but they had both been stung by bees on one occasion, making them believe that the bees had been assigned to guard Madame's privacy. In any case, he had never been invited inside and would have been scared to go in uninvited. But now thoughts of Marigot made him forget all his earlier fears.

He could see light glowing from the front window, so he assumed someone had to be home. He tapped on the door and waited awhile. Then suddenly a girl's voice called "Coming!" and the door opened to reveal Marigot, her head wound in a white turban and a long sarong tied over her breasts. At first he was alarmed, that she might also be involved in voodoo and was dressed in some sort of traditional garb.

"Sorry," she said. "I was in the shower. Had you been knocking long?"

"No, I just got here," he said with relief. "Your mother's still supervising dinner down at the main house."

"Yes, she is, isn't she?" Marigot said with that delightful Caribbean lilt. "You'd better come inside, then, hadn't you?"

She led the way into a living room. He had heard

rumors about Madame de Gaulle's living room, but nothing had prepared him for this: In the middle of one wall was a black-draped picture of the famous French general, on another his uniform. There were framed letters and photos, de Gaulle with Churchill, de Gaulle with Stalin and Roosevelt ....

"Holy cow!" Will exclaimed. "There's a lot of history here."

Marigot wrinkled her nose. "Too much history, if you ask me. I mean, even if she did know him, well, he's dead and gone, isn't he? And we're alive ...."

"I'm leaving in the morning," he said awkwardly. "I couldn't go without saying good-bye."

"I should think not," she said. "I was waiting for you to show up."

"I wasn't sure about coming here."

"It would hardly be right for me to come looking for you," she said bluntly.

"I hate the thought of going away again," he said. "Four months seems so awfully long."

"I expect you'll find enough to keep you busy," she said dryly.

"I swear I won't look at another girl," he said.

"I'll bet!" she replied.

"What will you do? Will you be here when I come back?"

"I might," she said. "On the other hand, I might not. I'll have to see what comes up."

He came closer to her. "Don't go, Marigot," he whispered. "I couldn't bear to come back and find you gone."

She tossed her head proudly. "You'll forget me in ten minutes when you get back to the States," she said, her eyes teasing him.

"I won't. You know I won't," he said. "As if I could ever forget you."

"You did for ten years."

"That's not fair. We were both little kids."

"And now we're a man and a woman," she said solemnly. "No more swimming races and wrestling matches, Will. We have much more important things on our minds."

She came up to him and slid her arms around his neck, pulling his lips down to meet hers. Her back was still damp from the shower, and she smelled so fresh, like a garden after spring rain. His hands moved down her back, seeking to inch down her sarong, which loosened and fell to the ground.

"Oh, Marigot," he murmured, his eyes feasting on her smooth dark flesh.

"Not here," she whispered. "Anyone could see us."

She took his hand and led him through to a small, dark bedroom. The only furniture was a bed and a white chest, but Will didn't even notice what the room looked like. He felt as though his body were on fire.

"This is so right," he whispered as he lowered himself on to her.

When it was over, she looked up him with smoldering eyes. "Now you won't forget me when you go back to the States," she said simply. And he hadn't forgotten. There wasn't a minute when she wasn't in his mind, when his body didn't ache for her again.

"The usual route of the Basque sheep herders through the Sierra Nevada ..." said the professor.

In his notebook Will wrote *Marigot*, over and over.

Laetitia Gambetti turned the key silently in the lock and let herself into the apartment. She held her breath as she tiptoed across the floor to the kitchen. No sound came from the baby's room. Thank heaven he was still asleep, or he might have woken Joseph. She knew she had taken a big risk in slipping out like this to see Robert. Her mother was feeling under the weather and couldn't take the baby at the last minute, but she didn't want Robert to think she had let him down. She had deliberately not given Robert her address or phone number for his own safety, and she hadn't taken his either. They had met six times now, and each time they planned the next meeting: always in a different place at a different time, so nobody could get suspicious. Once it had been at Grand Central, once at the bus terminal, today in the lobby of the Pierre hotel: anywhere they could blend in with crowds and one of Joseph's Mafia associates wasn't likely to see them.

She knew she shouldn't be doing this. It wasn't the breaking of her marriage vows that she minded. The meetings had been quite pure anyway. The closest they had come to physical contact was holding hands beneath a table, and once he had pressed her fingers to his lips before she climbed out of the taxi. What she feared was putting Robert in danger. She knew that killing came easily to her husband. She thought he actually enjoyed it. He was always animated and excited when he came home from killing.

She knew where he'd been … he usually woke her and made love roughly to her. These nights left her battered and bruised inside and out.

Every time she met Robert she told him that she couldn't see him again, and every time he would gaze at her with such longing and tenderness in his eyes that she knew she couldn't live without him. He had promised to take her away. Laetitia couldn't believe it would ever happen, but she dared to hope. If anyone could save her, Robert could. He radiated cool, efficient confidence. He seemed to be rich and he lived far, far away in the Caribbean. She began to dream that it might come true. If only she could get down to St. Martin, then Joseph could never harm her again.

The meeting with Robert had been wonderful. They had time for only a brief cup of coffee together, but he had told her he loved her and she believed it. She had stopped off on the way back to grab some groceries to make her trip seem legitimate. She put these on the counter now, then took the coffeepot over to the sink so that Joseph would have fresh coffee when he woke up. He was very particular about fresh coffee. Sometimes in restaurants he'd fling the coffee away if it tasted stale. Of course they always knew who he was in the restaurant and didn't make any sort of fuss. Joseph enjoyed that too. He liked his power.

As she began running water, a voice behind her made her jump. "Where the hell you been?"

She spun around guiltily to see Joseph standing in the doorway, still unshaven and in silk pajamas but wide awake. "I asked you a question," he repeated. "I said, where the hell you been? I woke up and I wanted coffee and you weren't here."

"I just had to go out for a few things," she said, looking at him defiantly. Maybe bluffing it out was the best way, she thought.

"Go out for a few things, eh?" he said, his lip curling in a snarl. "I'll tell you what you went out for. You were with some guy."

"What are you talking about? Go ask Mr. Rossini at the corner store."

"And Frankie saw you with some guy at the restaurant in the Pierre hotel," Joseph said, his eyes angry and gloating at the same time. "He called me right away because he thought I should know. He's a good friend, Frankie. He keeps an eye on my interests."

"And he made a mistake," she said. "I wasn't with anyone in a hotel."

"He didn't make a mistake," he said. "He described to me exactly what you were wearing. And he described the guy too—said he was a smooth-looking type in a dark suit."

"Oh, him," Laetitia said with an attempt at a light laugh. "That was just someone I used to know. We bumped into each other on Park Avenue and we talked for a few minutes."

Joseph's face was turning red. "What do you mean, used to know? You didn't know anyone before I met you. You were a little nothing."

"I used to know Roberto," she said. "His family lived down the street from us. He used to go to my church. Now he's a student at Yale and he was up in town for the day. We talked. What's so wrong with that?"

"Because I didn't give you permission to talk to no Yale guy, that's why," he said. "You don't talk to nobody unless I tell you to." The blow was quite unexpected and sent her sprawling. The coffeepot fell to the floor and glass and water flew everywhere.

She was sobbing quietly, still crouched on the floor. "And I'll tell you something else," he yelled, his face almost purple with rage now. "If you try and two-time me, you're going to wish you were dead! And so is the guy, understand me?"

From down the hall came a frightened whimpering.

"Now see what you've done," she said, sitting up and holding her cheek. "You're upsetting the baby."

"I'll upset the baby all right if you don't do as you're told," he said to her. "I'll make him real upset."

"You wouldn't hurt your own child!" she said, her anger taking over from fear.

He looked at her with disgust. "I can make a dozen more just like him," he said. "Which reminds me ...."

She inched away across the floor as he came toward her.

"It's about time we had another," he said. "My cousin Vinnie's already got six and his wife's not much older than you. What's the matter with you—only one kid? Everyone is starting to think there's something the matter with me, and I don't like that."

"I thought we agreed to wait until Joey was older," she said, her eyes trying to defy him with a boldness she didn't really feel.

"I changed my mind," he said. "I doubt your friend would find you so attractive with a big belly on you. Come here."

"No, Joseph," she said. It turned into a scream as he grabbed her by the hair.

"Shut up." This time it was an open-handed slap, but it sent her reeling and brought tears of pain to her eyes. He pushed her back roughly on the floor and lifted up her skirt. She turned her head away and felt tears running down her cheek. She blocked everything out until it was over, and, still crying herself, went to comfort her child.

Robert Philips came up out of the subway into bright spring sunshine. It was one of those clear and mild days that make you decide New York is a pretty place after all. The wind was scented with blossoms and everyone seemed to have dressed in bright colors in honor of the weather. Robert sniffed the wind appreciatively as he strode out toward the meeting place. He couldn't wait to see Contessa and tell her the news. He was amazed himself at how much progress he had made in a week.

He had been very shaken by their last meeting. She had slipped up to him in Macy's, her head tied up in a scarf, hiding all that beautiful hair.

"I can stay only a minute," she had whispered. "I think someone is following me."

They began to ride the escalator up together.

"You go down the back elevator and I'll come down the front one and we'll meet outside, " Robert said. "That way we'll give him the slip."

"There might be more than one of them," she said. He noticed the tremble in her voice and looked at her more closely. There was an ugly bruise down the left side of her face and her lip was swollen.

"He did that to you?" he demanded.

"And he's threatened to do far worse if I see you again," she said. "I had to come one last time to say good-bye."

The escalator arrived at the next floor and they stepped out to a bright display of women's spring clothing. "I'm not going to say good-bye, Contessa," Robert said. "I said I'd get you out of this, and I will. It's just going to take a little time, that's all."

"But you don't understand," she said, and he saw a tear trickle down her cheek. "He's threatened to harm Joey if I see you."

"Harm his own child? What kind of man is he?"

"He's a monster," she said, "but he's a powerful monster. He has contacts all over the city—all over the country, for all I know. If he finds out who you are, you won't be safe either. So please, for both our sakes, don't try to see me again."

They walked quickly across the floor and stood waiting for the back elevator. "I'm going to see you again, Contessa," he said. "Any risk would be worth taking for you. But I'll need a little time. I've got to find somewhere where you can hide out while I work on getting you a divorce."

She shook her head. "It will never work. It's impossible. He'll find me wherever I go."

"Not once you get to St. Martin," Robert said. "It's a small island and we know everybody. One word to the immigration people and they'll never let him land. You'll be safe, I promise you."

"If only that could be," she said, her eyes shining

through her tears. "If only it were possible."

"It will be, trust me," he whispered. "It will be a few weeks before I see you again anyway, because I've got finals at school. Maybe your husband will relax and think you've given me up. Shall we say same time, two weeks from today?"

"Where?"

"How about by the carriages opposite the Plaza on Central Park South? I'll do what I can to talk to my lawyers and have answers for you by then."

Then he gave her hand a squeeze and pushed her into the open elevator while he walked back through the store.

That had been one week earlier and Robert had tried to fit in visits to the lawyers in spite of last-minute cramming and final exams. After all the money his father had poured into his education, he would not be pleased if Robert failed now. So he pushed himself mercilessly, hardly sleeping or eating, trying to take care of both his obligations. Now the final exams were over and he had done well enough to pass. His young lawyer, a man without ties to his father's business, had given him helpful advice on getting a quickie divorce. He had also found a friend who would lend him an old converted barn in the middle of the Connecticut countryside where Contessa and her son could hide away.

During his absence the trees in Central Park had filled in with leaves. The cherry trees were a white froth of blossom and spring flowers bloomed in the beds. It seemed as if every New Yorker had caught spring fever. Children ran squealing ahead of parents, carrying kites or balls. Parents carried picnic baskets. Men had removed jackets. Robert smiled fondly at them all. It seemed unbelievable that he would soon be one of those fathers who held a son's tiny hand or carried him high on his shoulders. To be sure, it would not be his own son, but he didn't care. He was sure he would learn to love little Joey as much as he adored his mother, and in time there would be sons of their own. Robert felt suddenly very grown-up and proud—he was finally a man.

The horse-drawn carriages were doing a brisk trade with the first tourists of the season. Robert stationed himself on a bench behind them and watched the horses move off at an unhurried pace. He glanced at his watch. Any moment now she'd be coming toward him, her red hair flowing out behind her as she ran. His pulse quickened in anticipation.

Minutes passed and there was no sign of her. He waited a half hour and then an hour. Robert walked around, making sure she wasn't waiting for across the street. By late afternoon he finally had to admit that she wasn't coming. She hadn't been able to get away.

He rode the train home, his heart heavy with despair. He composed a personal ad for the *New York Times*. It read: Contessa. I'll be at the cleaners every day until you appear. Love you, Rob.

CHAPTER 7

Laetitia ran up the stone steps to her parents' apartment on the third floor and rang the bell impatiently. Her mother opened it and looked at her with surprise.

"Why, Laetitia, you're back early," she said. "I thought you were out for the day."

"No, just while I did my errands," Laetitia said. "Is Joey awake?"

"Joey?" Her mother's face was confused. "Joey's not here. Joseph came for him this morning, right after you dropped him off. He said you were waiting down in the car. Aren't you all going out of town for the day with friends?" A look of horror began to spread over her face. "That wasn't true?"

"No, Mama."

"Mother of God," the older woman said, crossing herself. "And the boy's not at home?"

"I don't know. I haven't been home yet. I just pray he is. I can't understand why Joseph would have come for him ...."

"Run home now and see," Laetitia's mother said. "Call me as soon as you know. I won't have a moment's peace until I find out."

"Nor I, Mama," Laetitia said. She fled down the stairs again and hailed the first taxi that passed.

She could hear the television going as she let herself into her own apartment, screams and laughter from a game show.

"Joseph?" she called. She glanced into little Joey's room on her way to the living room. The room was completely empty. Joey's furniture, his crib, even his toys were gone. "No!" she screamed in horror. She rushed through to the living room. Joseph was lying back on the sofa with a can of beer in his hand, grinning at the antics on the game show. She ran up to him and pounded him with her fists. "What have you done with him?"

He sat up and gave her a long, slow smile.

"You didn't learn your lesson very well, did you?" he said. "You saw that guy again. I warned you once. I don't warn people twice."

"If you've harmed him, so help me I'll kill you with a kitchen knife," she screamed.

"He's okay, so far," Joseph said calmly. "I've taken him somewhere for his own safety. I decided you weren't a fit mother, the way you're carrying on. I don't want the kid growing up around a tramp like you."

She ignored the insult. It was futile to deny it. "Bring him home, Joseph," she pleaded. "I'll do what you want if you just bring him home."

"You broke your word before," he said. "How do I know you won't break it again?"

"I promise. I swear to God, Joseph. Bring my baby back home and I'll do anything you want."

He began to laugh. It struck her that he was enjoying

every moment of this. If only she had a gun. If only it was in her hand right then. She'd have no trouble at all squeezing the trigger and putting an end to her misery.

"Anything I want, eh?" he said. "Okay. Go get a pen and a piece of paper and sit down."

She obeyed him. He waved the beer can in her direction, like an orchestra conductor. "Okay, now write what I tell you.

"Dear Robert," he dicated.

He laughed when he saw her shocked face. "Hey, stupid, " he said, "did you think I wouldn't be able to find out who he was? I've got connections all over, you know. I even have his address …. Mr. Robert Philips at Yale. My, we are moving up in the world, aren't we? Felt the urge for a little class?"

"What are you going to do to him?" She was shaking now.

"Nothing, if you write what I tell you, because he won't be around no more." He waved the can again. "Dear Robert.

"I am writing to you to tell you that I won't be seeing you anymore." He paused, savoring her face as she wrote those words. "I have decided that it is my husband I really love and want to spend my life with. I was happy with him until you showed up and I don't want my life disturbed ever again. So please, don't try to contact me. We patched up our differences and are having another baby together.

"Sincerely, Mrs. Joseph Gambetti."

He got up from his seat. "Got that? You better not have changed one word."

"I didn't change anything," she said. "Now can I have my baby back?"

"Sure," he said. "We'll go get him now and drop this off in the mail on the way."

She slid into the car beside him and they drove out of the city, heading along the Hudson toward upstate New York. "Why did you have to take him so far away?" she asked. "He's with friends, isn't he? You know how scared he is of strangers? And you left his blanket with him? He won't sleep without his blanket."

Joseph didn't answer but kept his eyes on the road. Along a rural country road he turned in between tall gates and pulled up at an imposing brick colonial house. There was a brass plate beside the door. It read Peacehaven Sanitarium.

"Why did you bring him to a place like this?" she demanded. "This place is for sick people. He might catch something."

"Oh, no," Joseph said, talking to her for the first time. "This is strictly for diseases of the mind."

He honked the horn. Immediately two attendants in white coats came out and took Laetitia by the arms. "Come on in, Mrs. Gambetti," they said. "You'll be taken care of here. We're going to make you well."

"Let go of me," she shouted, suddenly afraid. "There's nothing wrong with me. I've come for my son."

Joseph nodded at the attendants. "She still thinks she has a kid," he said. "I hope you can do something for her."

"What are you talking about?' she screamed, trying to free herself from the iron grip on her arms. "Joseph, what are you saying? Why are you doing this to me?"

He looked at her, his eyes triumphant. In an evil whisper he said, "You didn't think I'd let you get away with this, did you? After this, maybe you'll have learned your lesson."

He dismissed the attendants and they dragged Laetitia screaming up the steps. The door clanged shut behind her. She was hustled down a long, antiseptic hallway and into a small white room at the end. As the door closed behind her, a figure stepped out of the shadows.

"Relax, Mrs. Gambetti," he said. "Just a tiny prick and you'll feel better. It won't hurt a bit, I guarantee it."

Laetitia struggled as the needle stuck her arm, and seconds later she was unconscious.

Laetitia opened her eyes and tried to focus on the window. Green trees swayed in the wind and she could hear birds singing. On either side of the window were the white walls of a small, narrow room without decoration. She tried to remember where she was and why she was there … something to do with being sick? Sick in the mind? Needles in her arm. A long sleep … she struggled with memories that hovered on the fringe of her consciousness. Then names began to return—Joey … Joseph … and Robert. It was something to do with these three that had put her there. Gradually memories began to make sense. She was there because of Robert. Her husband and taken Joey away and she was a prisoner!

She had no idea how long she had been there. She spent day after day in a nightmarish state. As soon as she was awake enough to take in her surroundings, she was given another injection. For all she knew, she might have been there for months, or even years. The bright light hurt her eyes and she closed them again. She must think quickly while she still had the power to think. She had to get out of there somehow. Groggily she climbed out of bed and staggered over to the window. It was on the second floor and barred. How could she possibly escape?

"He's not going to get the better of me," she decided. "I will get out of here and find my child."

Any fear she might have had of Joseph had turned into cold anger at this despicable trick. She was determined never to see him again. But she knew that escape wasn't going to be easy. She needed to plan carefully and she needed a clear head to think. That was hardly possible if they kept on giving her injections. She heard footsteps in the hall outside and quickly lay back in bed, feigning sleep. Two male nurses came in. She lay there breathing deeply. When they straightened her sheets, she murmured and turned over.

"Boy, is she ever out of it," one said to the other.

That gave her an idea. Maybe they wouldn't inject her again until she woke up. She feigned sleep all that day, and when a doctor came by that evening, one of the nurses said, "She hasn't stirred all day. Do you think the dose might be too strong?"

"I'll check on it," the doctor said, and left without giving her a shot.

Laetitia began to feel hopeful for the first time. Her head was becoming clearer by the minute. Now, if only she could find an ally, someone on the staff who would believe her story. Through half-closed eyes she watched each per-

son who came into her room all the next day. She was
rewarded when a young doctor she didn't remember seeing
before entered her room. His name tag said Carlomagno.
An Italian—someone who might understand! As he picked
up her arm to inject her, Laetitia opened her eyes and
looked at him. "Please help me," she whispered.

"I am helping you," he said softly. "This medicine is
going to make you feel better."

"But you don't understand," she said, her eyes pleading
with him. "I'm not sick. I'm being kept here by my husband. I'm a prisoner here." She put her hand on his arm. If
ever there were a time when she needed every ounce of
her beauty and sex appeal, it was now. She had to make
him listen, or she'd never get out of there. "Look," she said,
desperate to convince him before he changed his mind and
gave her the shot, "I know it sounds bizarre, but I beg
you—just one favor. Just two minutes of your time. I can
prove that I'm as sane as you are. If you'd only take the time
to check the facts, you'd know I was telling the truth."

She could see he was beginning to weaken. "Why
would your husband do something like you suggest?" he
asked.

"Because I was seeing another man. He's very jealous,"
she said. "You're Italian. You know what Mafiosi are like."

A look of alarm crossed his face. "Your husband is
Mafioso?"

She nodded. "He works for the Mancini family. That's
obviously how he was able to leave me here … and I've no
idea where they've taken my child."

"But there isn't really a child," he said gently.

"Of course there's a child," she said impatiently. "Check the registry of births and deaths. My son Joey was born July 18, 1965, in St. Mary's Hospital. Check on that. It won't take you long. And find out what you can about my husband, Joseph Gambetti. That should tell you all you need to know."

He stared at her long and hard. "Please, I beg you," she said. "Someone here has to find out the truth and help me."

He nodded solemnly. "Very well, " he said. "I'll do what you ask."

After he'd left, Laetitia lay staring at the window, hardly daring to hope this doctor would keep her secret. She listened intently to every footstep passing in the hall outside. When a nursing assistant came with her evening meal, Laetitia pretended to be too tired to eat. Finally, hours after dark, her door opened and Dr. Carlomagno came in. He sat on her bed. "I believe you," he said simply. "Your son's birth checks out and I'd rather not know what I've learned about your husband." He paused while she held her breath. "I want to help."

Tears of joy ran down Laetitia's cheeks. "Thank God," she whispered.

"This isn't going to be easy," the young doctor said. "I've no desire to get on the wrong side of the Mafia. We'll have to make it look like you escaped without help."

She nodded. "I understand. But I must have my clothes. I'd be caught in a moment if I'm dressed like this."

"I'll see what I can do," he said, and he gave her a warm smile. But as he left, his face clouded over with worry.

The next morning he appeared in her room with a

white-draped tray. "Your clothes," he said quickly, "with your wallet in the pocket." He glanced back at the door. "I might have an idea how you can get out of here. A woman down the hall is being discharged this morning. They've ordered a taxi for her. Now, if I order a second taxi, you could be waiting in the bushes somewhere close by. You can discreetly get into the taxi. The gate staff will think you're the patient who is going home and let you pass."

"But I have to get out of the building somehow. They'd grab me as soon as I leave this room."

He nodded. "I think I took care of that. There's a white lab coat here. Put it on and walk briskly down the hall. Nobody will challenge you if they see a nurse's coat. There is a pretty big turnover of staff among the nurses here. Go down the back stairs and out the door at the bottom. You'll be in back of the house and you'll have to make your own way around to the front, but there are bushes where you can hide." He shrugged. "It's the best I can come up with, apart from calling the police, which could be disastrous for us all."

Her eyes filled with tears and the lump in her throat made it difficult to speak. "You've been wonderful," she said. "I don't know how to thank you."

He looked embarrassed. "Good luck," he said. "I'll be thinking of you."

He left her then and she had to wait patiently, hardly sleeping all night. She worried that someone would find the clothes she had hidden under her mattress or a nurse would notice that she wasn't fully drugged. She played her part perfectly as the morning staff fed her breakfast and washed her. Then, as soon as they had gone, she dressed and pulled on the white lab coat over her clothes. After that it was all too easy. No one appeared as she walked down the hallway, down the back stairs, and out through the door. When the taxi arrived, she appeared around the corner of the building and got in. "The train station please," she said, trying to remain calm.

The gates opened and the taxi drove out. Laetitia thought the countryside had never looked more beautiful. She resisted the urge to look back, just in case they were being followed. But before long they were pulling into a small town. She was on the platform and then on a train bound for New York. She could finally breathe a sigh of relief.

As the train sped on, she thought about Joey. Looking for her son in New York would be impossible. It would do no good to contact the police. Joseph was, after all, his legal father and she was terrified that he'd again be able to convince them that she was insane. She wouldn't go to her family either. As soon as news of her escape reached Joseph, her mother's house would be watched. She had to act very, very fast and to think very clearly.

Where would Joseph hide a three-year-old child? Joey wasn't always the easiest kid in the world. It would have to be somewhere where neighbors wouldn't notice his crying, where he would feel at home. Then it came to her: If she was safely in a sanitarium, he wouldn't really have to hide the child. The easiest thing would be to leave the boy with a member of his own family. She recalled something Joseph had said during one of their many arguments. "My cousin Vinnie already has six and his wife's not much older than you," he'd shouted.

That must be it! Who would notice another crying kid among Vinnie's six? As soon as she reached Manhattan, she caught a subway and headed out for Vinnie's house in Queens. Joey just had to be there. Surely she knew enough about Joseph by now to understand the way his mind worked? The house was like all the others on Maple Street: old, peeling paint, steps up to a front porch. No one was outside today, but a car was parked in front of the house. She didn't think Angelina went out much. Where could she go with four toddlers? Laetitia quietly looked around the house and found a perfect place to watch and wait. Although she was hidden from view behind a fence, she could hear sounds of children coming from inside. But nothing she could hear sounded like Joey.

At last she was rewarded. The back door opened and a whole brood of children ran out.

"Play nicely now," Angelina called from inside the kitchen.

Laetitia peeked through the cracks in the fence and saw four little boys. Her heart lurched when she saw that one of them was Joey. He was paler than when she last saw him, and dressed in clothes that were probably his cousin's hand-me-downs, but he seemed happy enough. He ran across the yard on his chubby little legs when the oldest boy yelled, "Come on, we're going to build a fort."

"Yeah," Joey cried, "build a fort!"

Laetitia waited, almost bursting with impatience until they settled down to play. She hoped that Angelina wasn't watching them from inside. The boys were playing nicely together, dragging branches and boards to make their fort along the side fence. Joey was trying to be extra helpful, handing them pieces of wood that they always rejected. At last she decided the moment was right. She hoisted herself over the fence and landed heavily on the other side. The boys looked up, surprised.

"Hey, it's Aunt Laetitia," the oldest boy said. "What are you doing here? How come you came in this way?"

Of course they hadn't been told the truth. They thought it was natural that she should come visit. Giving them a convincing smile, she said, "I've come to take Joey home. Thanks for playing with him so nicely."

She took Joey's hand. Joey struggled to pull away. "I don't want to go home yet. I want to build a fort," he said.

"We'll build another fort soon," she promised. She hadn't expected resistance to come from her own son. She had pictured him throwing himself sobbing into her arms.

"No, now!" Joey shouted.

The noise was enough to bring Angelina from the kitchen. "Hey, what's going on, guys?' she demanded. She appeared in the doorway, her broad frame having expanded with six births and already showing signs of another one on the way. "Are you guys bothering Joey?" Then she caught sight of Laetitia.

"What are you doing?" she demanded. "Joseph said that you were sick … what's going on?'

"I'm perfectly well, thank you," Laetitia answered civilly, "and I've come to take my son home." As she spoke, she swept the protesting child up into her arms, bundled him over the back fence, then scrambled over herself.

"Wait, you can't do that. Come back here. You're supposed to be crazy!" Angelina yelled after her. She waddled into the yard, but she was too heavy to clamber over the fence as Laetitia had done. "You come back here right now," she screamed, "or I'm calling the cops!"

"Go ahead, call," Laetitia yelled over her shoulder as she ran. "I think kidnapping is a felony in the state of New York!" She didn't think Angelina would have the nerve to call the cops, or that the cops could do anything if they found her with her own boy. But she was taking no chances. She fled down an alleyway, came out onto a busy street, and hopped onto a bus that was pulling away from its stop. When they pulled over at a subway station, she got off again. A few minutes later they were hurtling through the darkness of a tunnel. Joey clung to her, his arms wrapped around her neck.

"Mommy went away," he said.

"Mommy's back now, darling, and I'm never going away again," she promised. "Joey and Mommy are going on a fun trip to a nice place with a beach. You like playing on the beach, don't you?"

Suddenly she realized what to do next. She had been so focused on rescuing Joey that she had not even thought about where they would go. Robert—she had to find him again. But where was he? He must have finished his finals at Yale and received her letter by now. He would have had no incentive to stay in Connecticut. She made the decision to go straight to his home in the Caribbean. If he wasn't there, they'd know where to find him. He had said she'd be safe there, and she believed him.

She left the subway at the Kew Gardens station and took

a taxi to Kennedy Airport. By late afternoon they had landed in Miami and she went straight to the ticket counter to inquire about flights to St. Martin. It was then that she found out proof of citizenship was needed to enter what was a foreign country. She hadn't counted on that. How long did it take to get a passport? The airline clerk thought that they could rush one through in about a week, but suggested that a birth certificate would do as well.

Defeated for the moment, she tried calling Robert in Connecticut, on the off chance that he was still there, but the number had been disconnected. Then she risked calling her parents. She wasn't sure if Joseph could have a phone tapped, but she knew it was possible. She had to take the risk—she couldn't go anywhere without her birth certificate, and she was pretty sure it was still in her parents' lock box.

When she heard her mother's voice on the other end of the phone, Laetitia started to cry. She had been so strong, so brave for so long, and now she couldn't hold back the tears any longer. Joey clung to her with a worried look on his face.

"Where are you, honey? We've been so worried," her mother said. "Joseph said that you'd had some sort of breakdown and couldn't see anybody."

"Listen to me, Mom," Laetitia said quickly. "I have to talk fast. I'm fine. Joey's with me and he's fine, but we've got to get out of the country in a hurry. I can't explain why. You have my birth certificate, don't you? Send it to me at the main post office in Miami. I'll call you when it's safe, Mom. I love you both." Her hand was shaking as she hung up. If Joseph had been tapping the phone, he'd have someone in Miami onto her pretty soon. She'd better hide out. She took a taxi downtown and checked into a little hotel in the middle of the Cuban quarter. She hoped that nobody would look for her there. They were suspicious that she had no luggage with her but she found herself telling the truth to the proprietress, that she was running away from a husband who beat her, and the lady was immediately understanding. "Don't you worry," she said. "I'll keep an eye on the baby if you need to go out. I'll lend you some money if you need it to feed the child."

"That's very kind of you," Laetitia said. "Luckily I have my credit cards or I don't know what I would have done. I think I've got some time before he stops them." After Joey had a short nap, she took him out. She had intended to get only the essentials, but she suddenly realized that Joseph would be stuck with the bill. She headed for the best stores instead of the five and dime and bought them both new wardrobes. By the time she came home, she was almost laughing, imagining his face when he saw what she had done. He wasn't the only one who could get revenge, she thought. Then she remembered how terrible his type of revenge could be. He wasn't content to go shopping. He tortured and killed. And once again fear overtook her and she locked herself in her room.

On the third day Mrs. Rojas, the owner of the hotel, had her son go down to the main post office and return with Laetitia's birth certificate, plus five hundred dollars from her parents. They had included a note. "This is all we can spare at the moment, but let us know where you are, and we'll try and send you more." She wanted to cry again. Instead, she gathered Joey and their things and headed to the airport. A short while later they were on a plane headed toward the blue Caribbean.

CHAPTER 8

The 727 began to make its descent. Laetitia looked out the window and saw only clear turquoise water sparkling below her. She had never believed that water could really be that shade of blue. As the plane banked, she found herself staring at an island paradise. In the center was a shaggy mountain peak. There were tiny towns of red-roofed houses, a glistening lake at one end, and perfect white sand beaches outlining the island, with a line of surf breaking upon them.

"Oh," she said out loud. She had never imagined anyplace as lovely. Laetitia thought she had died and gone to heaven. After what she had been through, it was almost true. The plane banked again, the seat belt sign came on, and they touched down. "Welcome to Juliana Airport," the hostess said. "Local time is twelve-thirty and the temperature outside is eighty-five degrees. We hope you have a pleasant stay in St. Martin."

Laetitia scooped up Joey and followed other passengers down the steps of the plane into the brilliant sunshine. Soft-scented Caribbean breezes caressed her skin. Flowers grew wildly around the airport building. Beyond the small terminal she got a glimpse of blue water. After days on the run, the surroundings seemed to melt her tensions away. She glanced around at people standing on the tarmac, half expecting to see Robert's face. She knew it was illogical to think that he'd somehow know she was there, but she scanned the crowd anyway. She felt an absurd sense of disappointment when nobody came forward to meet them.

At last she was standing in the air-conditioned immigration hall.

"Address on St. Martin?" the official asked in a clipped Dutch accent.

"I don't have one yet," she said. "I'm probably going to be staying with Robert Philips. Do you know him?"

"Christof's boy? Of course I know him," the official said, "but I don't think he's here, is he?"

"I'd hoped he would be," she said. "Where would I find … uh … Christof?"

"Up at Plantation Rum," he said. "Take a taxi. It's only a few miles out of town." He glanced at the clock on the wall. "They'll break for lunch around now. I should try the house first."

"The house?'

"Yeah, the old plantation house. The driver will know it."

"Thank you," Laetitia said.

"We'll put him down as your contact address, then," the man said. "I'm not supposed to let you on the island without a return ticket or a hotel reservation, but Christof will no doubt vouch for you."

She collected her bags and bundled an exhausted Joey into a taxi. It was an ancient Studebaker. A sign on the window said air-conditioned, but the windows were open and the fan wasn't blowing any air. They drove out of town at a leisurely pace. Neat little Dutch-style houses were gradually replaced with Caribbean bungalows, hidden behind banana trees and bougainvillea hedges. The scenery grew more rural. Small farms sprang up every few feet along the road. Goats were tied to fence posts, and naked brown babies played on front porches. Then came the sugarcane fields, mile after mile, towering above the taxi on either side of the road.

"This is all Plantation Rum from here on," the driver said.

"And the Philips family owns it?" she asked.

"They own almost half the island," the driver said. "Mr. Philips is the biggest employer on either side."

Laetitia was more excited than impressed. She knew that Robert wasn't poor; his clothes and the way he spoke told her that. But she had never dreamed that she and Joey would be moving to a life of such riches. No wonder he talked of getting her the best lawyer money could buy and taking care of her and Joey. The Philipses were obviously as powerful here as the Mancini family was in New York. She really might be safe and protected from Joseph here.

The sugarcane fields ended abruptly and she got her first glimpse of Plantation House. It was an old-style Dutch planter's house from a grander era—long, low, and rambling with shady verandas and flowering creepers. Gardeners looked up as the taxi passed.

"Wait for me, please," she said. "I'm not sure yet if I'll be staying."

She left Joey sleeping in the car, and the luggage, and

walked up to the front door. It was opened by a regal-looking black woman.

"Yes?" she said, looking Laetitia up and down.

"I'm a friend of Robert Philips's," Laetitia said. "Is he here?"

"No, he's not," the woman said.

"Perhaps you know where I can find him? It's rather important."

"Sorry," the woman said. "I can't help you there. He's not on the island."

"Then may I speak to his father?" Laetitia asked.

"Mr. Christof is resting. He always takes a nap after lunch," the woman said with increasing impatience.

"I've just come from the States," Laetitia said, beginning to sound desperate. "It will take only a moment."

"What is it, Madame de Gaulle?" came a deep voice from the darkness of the house, and a gray-haired man appeared at the door. He was barefoot and wearing only shorts. Laetitia recognized him immediately as an older version of Robert.

"You must be Robert's father," she said. "I'm a friend of his from the States. I was hoping to find him here."

"Then I'm afraid you've made the journey for nothing," the man said not unpleasantly. "He's not home at the moment."

"Do you have any idea when he'll be coming home?" She was finding it hard to keep her composure now, and her voice trembled.

Christof spread his hands wide. "Your guess is as good as mine," he said. "All I have is a letter saying that he'd be taking some time off after his finals and seeing a little of the world before he comes back here to work. That could mean three weeks, three months, or three years, I imagine. He might not be in any hurry to come back and settle down to work at the factory. We got a postcard from Paris, but that's it so far."

"Oh," Laetitia said, the color draining from her cheeks. She had been so sure that she was at the end of her journey, close to safety.

"I'm sorry I can't be more helpful," Christof said. "Were you planning to stay on the island for long, Miss … uh? Because if you are, why don't you leave me your address and I'll get in touch with you if he comes back."

The way he looked at her said it all. He took in the luxuriant red hair and bright clothing and dismissed her as someone Robert had met at a beach or a disco. He was used to young women hanging around Robert. She was just another one of them and he was probably doing Robert a favor by giving her the polite brushoff.

"Thank you," she said, "but I'm not sure how long I'll be staying."

In a daze she stumbled back down the steps and into the taxi.

"Where to now, Madame?" the driver asked.

Laetitia had no idea. She could wait three weeks for Robert, but three months or three years? But then, she'd be as safe there as anywhere. "I need somewhere cheap to stay," she said. "Do you know of an inexpensive hotel?"

"Most of the hotels are pretty expensive here," the driver said, "but I tell you what. I think Mr. Sommers over at

Trade Winds has some bungalows on his property that he was talking of renting out. I don't think he'd charge much for one of them. You want to drive over and see?"

"Okay," she said. She was thinking that a bungalow would be a good idea. She could do her own cooking and it would be easier with Joey. They swung over the spine of the island in a series of hairpin curves and passed a sign saying YOU ARE NOW ENTERING THE FRENCH SIDE in three languages. There were no officials and no border. As they dropped down on the other side, there were fewer cane fields and more smallholdings with banana trees, papayas, and herds of goats.

As the taxi made its way up the long drive of the hotel, Laetitia was sure she'd never be able to afford any sort of accommodation they had to offer. Trade Winds looked magnificent with its white columns and palm trees and turquoise water beyond. The taxi driver sounded his horn as they came up the driveway and a young, very tanned man in white shorts came out. He had sun-streaked sandy hair and the beginnings of a blond beard. Laetitia was surprised by her reaction. She could definitely appreciate this man's attractiveness.

He looked at her with equal appreciation as she got out of the taxi. "Hi, welcome to Trade Winds. I'm Rick Sommers, the owner," he said, then seemed to recognize the taxi driver. "Hey, Theo, *comment ça va?*" he asked.

"Hi, boss. This lady needs a cheap place to stay, and I heard that you might be renting out those little bungalows."

"I was considering it," Rick Sommers said, "but they're not ready yet. We've used them only for staff until now. "

"I don't need anything fancy," Laeitita said quickly. "I just need a place to stay."

Rick shrugged. "Maybe by the end of the month. We've had so much else to do that the bungalows sort of got pushed aside."

He gave Laetitia a friendly smile, but this was the last straw for her. To have escaped the hospital, rescued her child, come so far, and done so much alone, finding nobody willing to help her was too much to bear! She had been so strong, so brave, but now she didn't think she could go on any longer. Without warning, tears started to well up in her eyes and trickle down her cheeks.

"Oh God," she said as she sat down on the edge of the cab, "I just can't take it anymore. I can't keep on going like this. There's no end." She covered her face in her hands. "I'm sorry," she muttered, trying to compose herself.

"Hey, it's okay," Rick said, gently putting his hand on her arm. He pulled her to her feet and steered her to a chair in the shade. He motioned for the driver to wait.

Hurriedly she tried to wipe her cheek with her fingers. "I don't normally behave like this. I don't know what you must think of me," she said. "I'm really not the hysterical type. It's just that I thought I'd finally be safe here."

"Safe from what?" Rick asked.

"I've been trying to get away from my husband," she said. "He took my baby from me, and was threatening me, and Robert was going to help me ...." She didn't have the energy to go on.

"Robert?"

"Yes, Robert Philips—do you know him?"

"Sure, I know Rob. We're childhood friends," he said.

"We met in New York," Laetitia said, "and he was so wonderful to me. Before I knew him I had no hope at all. I thought I'd be stuck in that terrible marriage, living in fear every day. But Robert gave me hope again. He promised he'd arrange for a divorce and then he'd take me to the island, where I'd be safe. I really began to believe that everything would be all right. But then my husband found out about him. He made me write a letter saying that I never wanted to see him again. Robert must have believed it, because he's left the States and his father doesn't know where he is or when he's coming home." She looked up helplessly at Rick. "I'm sorry. I don't know why I'm telling you all this. It's just that I've had to do so much alone—I had to sneak my little boy away from the people who were hiding him …."

"You've got a baby with you?" Rick asked.

She nodded. "He's sleeping in the car. He's only three years old. That's why the bungalow would have been perfect. He wouldn't disturb anybody." She got to her feet. "I'd better get going. I've already taken up enough of your time. You wouldn't happen to know of an inexpensive hotel, would you? Your hotel is lovely, but I'm sure I couldn't afford your rates."

"Wait a minute," Rick said. "I'm sure we can fix up something for you. The bungalows really need refurbishing, but if you don't mind furniture cast off from the hotel, I can have Aimee get one ready for you."

She turned to him, beaming with gratitude. "You'd really do that for me? Oh, Mr. Sommers. I can't tell you how much I appreciate it. "

Rick blushed. "Robert's like family," he said. "Any friend of his is a friend of mine."

A sudden bout of dizziness came over her, and she swayed. Instantly Rick caught her. "Hey," he said. "You'd better come back and sit in the shade. I'll bring you a cool drink."

"I have to get my son from the car," she said, protesting. "He's asleep."

"I'll get him for you," Rick said. He opened the taxi door and she heard him say, "Hi there, Tiger. Come on, let's go see your mom." And to her amazement he lifted Joey out without a word of protest. "Cute little guy," Rick said. "You just relax. I'll bring you both some fresh lime juice."

"You want me to unload the bags, boss?" Theo asked.

"Sure, Theo. Just leave them on the porch," Rick said.

As if in a dream, Laetitia sank into the pillows of the wicker chair. Rick returned with two tall glasses. "Here you are Mrs …."

"Just call me Contessa," she said, and smiled to herself.

"I'm Rick," Rick said. "No more of this Mr. Sommers nonsense. But tell me … uh … Contessa, do you really think your husband would be able to trace you all the way down here?"

She nodded, her eyes solemn. "He's with the Mafia, Rick," she said. "You'd be amazed what connections they have. I'm very afraid, even down here. So please. If anyone asks about me, tell them you haven't seen me."

"Okay," he said. "Now, if you've finished that drink, do you want to come see which bungalow we can put you in?"

Contessa settled in to life in the bungalow quickly. She'd walk to a little store that was close by in the morning, take Joey down to the beach or sit, watching him play in the shade of the big pine trees. Rick often stopped by to visit as he went about his chores. He seemed to like playing with Joey, and he would bring him back a toy every time he went into town.

"You must stop spoiling him, Rick," Contessa said.

"Since when did a thirty-cent ball count as spoiling?" Rick asked, laughing. "The poor kid hardly has any toys."

"He doesn't need toys. He's happy playing in the sand and the water," she said. "The life here agrees with him." And this was definitely true. Not only did the child look like a sturdy little native, he was waking less at night and having fewer crying spells.

"It seems to agree with you too," Rick said, letting his eyes roam appreciatively over her naked tanned shoulders and down over the jungle print sundress that seemed to be suspended like magic halfway down the magnificent domes of her breasts.

"All the same, I can't stay here forever," she said quickly because the intensity of his gaze was disturbing. She could sense him mentally undressing her. "My money won't last much longer, even though I'm sure you're charging me well under value for the bungalow. If only I could get in touch with Robert and let him know that I'm here."

"He really means a lot to you, doesn't he?" Rick asked.

"He's the most wonderful man I've ever met," she said simply. "I'd never met a man like him before. I didn't even know that men like him existed. He was so sweet to me,

Rick. So gentle, so caring. It broke my heart when I had to write that letter and I thought I'd never see him again."

"I see," Rick said. He cleared his throat. "Well, he has to come home eventually. Christof is grooming him to take over Paradise Rum someday and Robert isn't exactly the type to go bumming around Nepal or India, looking for the meaning of life."

Contessa smiled. "Yes, he takes life very seriously," she said. "I can't imagine what he was like as a child."

"Oh, always the cautious one," Rick said, grinning. "We were a threesome, Robert and his brother, Will, and I. Will and I are younger and we were always getting in scrapes. We'd climb a cliff, get stuck halfway and have to be rescued, and once we ate green bananas and got a terrible stomachache, but somehow Robert always managed to stay out of trouble."

"He was prepared to get into trouble to help me," she said. "I warned him about my husband and the Mafia, but he wouldn't give up on me. He told me he was willing to risk everything so we could be together."

"He really must have it bad, then," Rick said. "I don't ever remember Robert falling head over heels over a woman before."

"He adored me," Contessa said wistfully.

"And you?"

"I felt the same way about him."

Rick got to his feet. "I'll ask around and see if anyone has any idea how to get in touch with him," he said. "I better be getting back to the hotel. We're almost half full today, which is pretty much a record for us."

"Rick," Contessa called after him.

He looked back at her. "Thank you for Joey's gift," she said, "and for everything else you've done for me."

"Sure," he said, "No problem." He started toward the hotel, then seemed to think of something and turned back to her. "It must be pretty boring stuck out here all the time," he said. "I was planning to take the boat out tomorrow afternoon. Would you and Joey like to come along?"

"Boat, boat!" Joey yelled, jumping up and down. "Mommy, boat!"

Contessa smiled. "He seems to have answered for me," she said. "Thank you very much, if you're sure we'd be no trouble."

"No trouble at all," he said.

The next afternoon they set out in a sleek powerboat, skimming the ocean. A large cruise ship was steaming into port. They met its wake and Joey squealed with delight as they bounced over the series of waves. Contessa closed her eyes and felt the wind in her hair. She was determined to leave all her problems back on the land. For one afternoon she wouldn't worry about money, Robert, or Joseph. She stretched her legs out, feeling the spray cool them.

"Okay?" Rick asked, turning to her.

"Perfect," she said. "I can't remember when I last felt this relaxed."

"That's why I like boating. It puts your troubles in perspective."

"You have troubles too?"

"Plenty," he said.

"Like what?"

"The hotel, for one."

"The hotel? It's a beautiful place."

"It's a nightmare," he said. "It was my parents' dream. They built it and never imagined how much it would cost to keep up. Last year we had a hurricane here which did a lot of damage. We were just up and running again when they were killed in a plane crash."

"Oh, I'm very sorry."

"It's okay. I'm getting used to it," he said, "but suddenly I'm stuck with all these responsibilities, that money pit back on shore, and no time to myself. I used to imagine that I'd finish college and come back here to lead a pretty good life. You know? The playboy of St. Martin. Hang out on the beaches, go to clubs, always have a beautiful girl around …" He let his eyes linger on her again. "Of course, that part's been fulfilled now, only she happens to be someone else's girl."

"I'm sure you never have trouble meeting beautiful women," she said.

"I wouldn't if I had time. Since I've been stuck with the hotel, it's been a twenty-four-hour a day job."

"And you gave up your one free afternoon to take Joey and me out when you could have been picking up girls from that cruise ship."

"I like spending time with you and Joey," he said. He turned back to the little boy. "Hey, Joey, want to do some fishing?"

"Yeah, fishing," Joey said.

Rick cut the engine and the boat bobbed on the water as Rick opened a panel and pulled out fishing rods. He baited one line and threw it over the side. "Here, hold that," he said to Joey. "And if you feel a tug on it, don't let go. Just yell and we'll help you bring in the fish."

"Okay." Joey's eyes were solemn as he held on to the line.

"You want one too?" he asked Contessa.

"Sure. Anything to make the food budget go further," she said, laughing. Rick handed her a line. "You'd better put some suntan lotion on you," he said. "You'll burn easily out here."

He unpacked a bottle and handed it to her. She began to spread the lotion over her arms and naked shoulders, then down her long legs, conscious that Rick was watching her.

"Here," he said. "Turn around and I'll do your back."

The lotion felt cool and soothing. She could feel his fingers caressing her back in smooth, sensuous circles. She closed her eyes. It had been so long since a man had touched her, and Rick's fingers were firm and warm on her flesh. It made her feel like a woman again ... she didn't want him to stop. But abruptly he did.

"Did you get it all?" she asked.

"Just about," he said quickly.

"Do you want me to put some on you?"

"I never burn," he said, putting the lotion back in its cubby hole.

They sat in silence , watching the bobbing lines. Contessa could sense that the encounter had disturbed Rick as much as it had excited her. She could feel a current between them that hadn't been there before, as if they were both conscious of their closeness.

Then suddenly Contessa's line jerked in her hand. She

gave a little squeal and brought in a fish.

"Is it good to eat?" she asked as Rick took it off the hook for her.

"Sure. It's a flying fish. They're delicious," he said.

"I want to catch a fish," Joey said.

"You will," Rick answered.

"When?"

"Just be patient," Rick said. "I tell you what. I'll dive down and take a look at your bait for you. Make sure it's still there. Okay?"

"Okay."

Rick made eye contact with Contessa and winked as he picked the flying fish from the floor of the boat, then dove over the side with it. Joey tried to lean out to watch him. A few seconds later he appeared again. "Hey, Joey," he said. "It looks like you've got a fish on your hook. Didn't you feel it tugging?"

"No," Joey said.

"Well, reel it in and let's see."

Together they wound in the line. Contessa watched her son's excited face, and Rick's amused eyes as the flying fish appeared for a second time on a line.

"Look, Mommy, I caught one!" Joey screamed. "It's bigger than yours, right?"

"Much bigger," Contessa agreed. Her eyes met Rick's in a shared joke. He's nice, she thought. He knows how to make people happy .... And she found herself wondering if Robert never came back, how would she feel about Rick Sommers?

They didn't catch any more fish, so they pulled in the

lines and headed back to shore again. As they walked past the back terrace of the hotel, a New York newspaper lay open on a chair. Contessa glanced at it with interest. She had heard nothing from home since she arrived in St. Martin. It was as if New York had ceased to exist. Now hungry for news, her eyes scanned the front page headlines. Suddenly something caught her eye. She stood frozen on the terrace, Joey tugging at her hand, as she read:

In an apparent old-style-Mafia power play, five members of the Mancini crime family were massacred last night in an abandoned warehouse in Queens. The dead were identified as Frankie and John Verspucci, Raymond Vaio, Vic Del Grande, and Joseph Gambetti.

"Rick!" she screamed.

He spun around, running to her side. "What is it?"

She was pointing at the paper, unable to speak. "Look," she managed to stammer at last, "my husband's dead. Joseph Gambetti. He's dead. Do you know what that means? I'm free. I'm finally free."

Without warning she flung her arms around him, sobbing on his shoulder. Awkwardly he put his arms around her and patted her on the back like a child. "That's wonderful, Contessa. Now there's nothing to stop you from marrying Robert as soon as he comes back," he said.

CHAPTER 9

Laetitia lay sweating in the oppressive heat of her bungalow. All day a storm had been brewing and the air was hot and heavy. She had just drifted off to sleep when there was a thundering knock at her front door. As she sat up, she listened in horror as the blows continued until the door burst open and Joseph Gambetti walked in.

"Joseph," she screamed, "you're alive. It can't be. The newspaper said you were killed."

"Newspapers don't always get it right, do they?" he said, his white teeth flashing in the darkness of the cabin. "I've been looking all over for you, doll. And now I finally found you." He began to move toward her.

"What are you going to do, Joseph?' she sobbed. "Please don't hurt me. Don't hurt my baby."

"A little late for that now, wouldn't you say?" he said, still grinning. "You disobeyed me once too often, and now you got to pay the price. The Mancini family doesn't like it when someone disobeys them, do we, boys?"

Laetitia peered into the shadows and noticed that several more dark figures had entered the room. Each carried a gun.

Joseph brought out his own gun. "Nobody will ever know what happened to you, Laetitia," he said.

He raised the gun in her direction. The other men did the same. "No, no, please," she was sobbing. "Please, please, please …"

"Too late," Joseph said. "Okay, boys, get to it."

Gunfire exploded from all directions. As she was blown into a million pieces, Laetitia woke to the sounds of her own screams in the darkness of her own room. The cool, reassuring touch of her pillow reminded her she was safe. A dream— it had been a nightmare, not real.

She was just able to breathe again when there was another deafening crash, and, at the same time, a brilliant blue flash of light. Contessa clutched her pillow, her whole body shaking. First the dream and now this. She had always been terrified of storms. As a small child she'd run to her parents' bed, hiding her face against her mother's warm chest until the storm was over. Joseph had always laughed at her fear. Sometimes he'd deliberately go out when there was a storm, so that she'd be left in the apartment alone. She'd lie whimpering and trembling with a pillow over her head until he returned.

In a blind panic she stumbled out of bed, her heart hammering. She stood there, still clutching the pillow to her. Tropical rain had begun to cascade down in sheets and was hammering on her roof. The next flash of lightning revealed palm trees, tossed and turned by the wind as if they were part of a native island dance. Thunder shook the whole cottage.

It was followed almost immediately by the sound of knocking on her front door. Contessa gasped. This time she was awake and the knocking was real. Was it possible

Joseph was alive and coming to get her? Her one thought was to snatch up Joey and escape to the safety of Rick's bungalow. But she hadn't even reached his crib when the lock began to turn and the front door opened slowly. This time she was too terrified to scream.

Rick Sommers was finishing up some paperwork when the storm broke. He listened to the rain drumming on the tile roof and he prayed that the patch on the hotel roof would hold. He knew he should go check, but he was so tired. Another setback would be too much. "And if the patch is leaking, there's not much I can do," he told himself. He'd be crazy to go up on that roof in a storm like this.

A great crash of thunder was followed by the crack of a tree splintering and falling. He ran to open his door and stood surveying the wild scene. Palm fronds were down all over the lawn, but he couldn't make out which tree had fallen. Then he thought of Contessa and Joey in the bungalow next door. He'd better make sure they were all right.

He tapped on her door, but got no answer. Probably the noise of the storm had drowned out his knocking. So he took out his passkey and opened the door cautiously. He started when he saw a white figure in front of him. Contessa was standing in the middle of the floor, a look of sheer terror on her face. Before he could say anything, she turned and fled across the bungalow, fumbling desperately with the lock on the back door, then fleeing out into the night. Rick sprinted across the bungalow after her and caught her a few steps away from the house.

"Contessa! It's okay. It's only me, Rick," he yelled over

the storm. He could feel her whole body shaking.

Gradually she turned to face him and he saw the terror leave her eyes. "Oh, Rick," she gasped. "I thought it was Joseph. I thought he'd found me."

"Joseph's dead," Rick said. "Come back inside."

"No, he came. He was here," she protested as he led her back into the house. "It must have been a dream, but it was so real. Joseph came and the Mafia and they had found me and they all pointed guns at me and I woke up to find it was thunder and I'm terrified of storms …."

"It's okay. You're safe now," he said gently as he closed the door behind them.

"Hold me, Rick. I'm so scared," she whimpered.

He took her into his arms. He could feel her heart pounding against him through the flimsiness of her gown.

He stoked her wet hair. "It's okay. You're safe here," he soothed her. "Joseph is dead and nobody's going to harm you."

"Hold me tight, Rick," she murmured. "Don't let me go."

"I won't let you go," he said in a strangled voice. He could feel her breasts pressing against him, her cold, wet flesh against his making him hungry with desire.

She raised her face to his. "Rick, Rick," she murmured.

Suddenly he was kissing her with abandon and she was returning his passion, wrapping herself around him, her body already moving against him.

"Do you want me, Contessa?" he asked huskily.

"Yes, yes," she gasped. "God, how I want you …."

He carried her onto the bed. The wet nightgown came away to reveal her perfect body, the curve of her hips, the smooth hollow of her stomach. She was the most luscious, the most delectable woman he had ever seen. He would have liked to cover her body with slow kisses, but he couldn't wait a second longer. Neither could Contessa. She lay back and grasped for him, her fingernails digging into his back as she dragged him onto her.

"Yes, Rick, yes," she gasped, groaning with passion as they moved together, their mouths searching for flesh … she felt a surge of pain as he bit into her neck and she latched her lips onto his, forcing her tongue deep into his mouth. There was an explosion of fire. All the storms of the Caribbean night came together in a giant thunderclap as the lovers suddenly shuddered and then lay still, gasping.

For a long while neither of them moved. Then through the rumble of distant thunder and the drumming of rain came a child's high pitched cry: "Mommy, where are you?"

They sprang apart guiltily. "Right here, darling," Contessa said.

"I better go." Rick started to pull on his clothes.

She nodded and reached for her robe.

"You're okay now?" he asked.

"Yes, I'm okay now," she said.

"I'll see you in the morning, then," he said.

"Yes."

She gave him one brief, longing glance as she passed him to go to her child.

In the morning she woke to bright sunshine and the realization of what had happened the previous night. The lovemaking with Rick seemed more like a dream, and she wondered for a moment whether any of the events of the past night had been real. She got out of bed and looked at herself in the mirror. There was a red mark on her neck and her lips were bruised and swollen. She hadn't imagined any of it, then. It had all happened, every incredible second.

A few minutes later there was a tap on her door. She pulled on her robe and Rick came in, already showered and dressed in his official blue button-down shirt and khaki shorts.

"Hi," he said a little shyly.

"Hi."

"So you finally got to sleep."

"Yes, I did."

"That's good, then."

"You're a little tiger, you know that?" he said, laughing awkwardly. He opened his shirt to reveal a long scratch down his shoulder.

"You weren't exactly gentle yourself," she said, her hand going up to her neck and her lip.

"I'm sorry," he said.

They gazed at each other, their eyes remembering details. Then Contessa said, "Look, Rick, about last night ..."

He spoke at the same time. "I've been thinking, Contessa ... We really should talk about this ..."

They both stopped and smiled.

"I need to know how to think about this," Rick said at last.

She nodded. "I know. It sort of complicates things, doesn't it?"

"I felt very guilty afterward," Rick said.

"Me too."

"I mean, you're going to marry Robert. It was hardly fair …. We had no right." He looked at her imploringly. "You do still love him, don't you?"

She sank back onto the bed. "I don't know," she said. "I think I do. Of course I do. You're right, Rick, we shouldn't have let this happen and we won't again. We should stay away from each other."

"Is that what you really want?"

Contessa looked up at him with tears in her eyes.

"Yes," she said at last. "It's what I really want."

"Okay, then," he said slowly, "but tell me you thought it was as fabulous as I did."

She looked at him steadily. "It was incredible. I—I'd only ever been with Joseph before, and it was never … you made me feel … it was incredible," she repeated, at a loss for words. "Is it always as good as that? Will it be like that with Robert?"

Rick laughed. "I shouldn't imagine so. I would think that Robert is the type who has to read the manual first … but it's always that good with me."

"You're so modest."

"No, just honest …" Then he shook his head. "If you want to know the truth, it's never been like that before for me either. Never, and I've been with my share of women. With you I was on fire."

"And yet we mustn't think of it after today, Rick. I couldn't face Robert if you and I had been carrying on behind his back."

"I understand. We'd better keep away from each other,

then. No more boat rides or I won't be able to keep my hands off you."

"No more boat rides," she agreed. "Maybe I should try to find somewhere else to live. Do you think I could get a maid's job at one of the big hotels?"

Rick smiled. "I hardly think Robert would be pleased if he arrived home to find his future bride was a maid on the island. He's somewhat of a snob, I think. He takes his status at Paradise Rum pretty seriously."

"I hope he comes back soon, then, or I'll definitely need to get a job."

"I hope he comes back soon, for both our sakes," Rick said. "It's not going to be easy, knowing you're in the next bungalow at night."

"No, it's not going to be easy," she said, "but we'll manage for Robert's sake, won't we?"

"Sure, for Robert's sake," he said. "I have to get back to the hotel, Contessa. Let me know if you need anything."

"Good-bye, Rick," she whispered. Her eyes followed him all the way across the lawn and up the steps into the hotel.

After that they made sure they kept a polite distance from each other, but Contessa couldn't get him out of her mind. At night her body ached for him, and she found herself standing in the darkness at her window, watching his silhouette behind the blinds of his bungalow. She was tempted so many times to run over to him again, and each time she forced herself to think of Robert and put Rick out of her mind.

One night she woke to find a full moon streaming in through the open window. The air was scented and soft and all around tree frogs called peep-peep in high, chiming voices. She got out of bed and stood on the front porch, taking in the moon-drenched beauty of the scene, the gracefully swaying palm trees, the song of a night bird, the distant rumble of surf breaking on the shore. She found herself truly at peace and completely sure that coming to this island had been right. Her troubles were behind her.

When she saw a figure moving in the trees, she stiffened, terrified for a second that the Mafia had tracked her down after all. But then the figure came forward into the moonlight and she saw that it was Rick. He'd been for a swim and had just a towel wrapped around him. He was halfway between her house and his when he stopped and stood, gazing at the sky, as enraptured with the moonlight as she had been. She couldn't resist any longer. She began to walk toward him across the soft, springy grass.

"Rick?" She called his name softly.

He turned toward her and his eyes lit up at the sight of her. "You couldn't sleep either?"

He shook his head. "I went down to the ocean to cool off. I've been doing that a lot lately."

"Are we fooling ourselves, Rick?" she asked. "I've tried to get you out of my mind, but I can't."

"And I can't stop thinking about you. I see your face, feel your body, day and night, Contessa."

Step by step they moved toward each other, as if being pulled by an invisible force.

"I've been thinking that Robert might not come back for years," she whispered.

"And he might have found another woman by now," Rick added.

"So all our noble sacrifice might be for nothing," she whispered. She was close enough to touch him now. "And that would be a terrible waste, wouldn't it?"

"A terrible waste," he whispered back.

With a cry of desire they fell into each other's arms and sank to the grass together. Their lovemaking was just as urgent and passionate as the first time, leaving them both spent, gasping.

"I'm not going to let you go again," he said, tenderly stroking her beautiful mane of hair. "We belong together, Contessa. Robert will have to understand that if he comes back. I'll have your things moved into my bungalow in the morning."

She gazed at him with adoring eyes. "All right, Rick," she said. "It doesn't make sense to fight this any longer."

He escorted her back to her bungalow, where she fell into a blissful sleep. She woke to bright sunshine and to Joey whispering in her ear.

"Mommy, Mommy, I'm hungry. When are we gonna have breakfast?" he demanded.

Contessa laughed and slipped on a sundress. "We'll walk down to the store and get milk now," she said.

As she passed Rick's cabin, she saw movement inside.

"Hi, Rick. Did you sleep well?" she called.

But Aimee's face looked out instead of Rick's. "Oh, hello there, Miss Contessa," she said. "Mr. Rick's not here. Doesn't look like he slept in his bed last night either. Probably down in town with a lady friend," she laughed.

"That's Mr. Rick for you. A great one for the ladies. Never keeps the same one for more than a few days, and then a new one catches his eye. Always like that as a little boy too. Had a favorite toy and carried it everywhere with him, then a week later he dropped it for something new and never touched it again."

"I see," Contessa said, wishing Aimee would stop talking.

But Aimee kept chuckling. "He's a sweet boy, Mr. Rick, and a real charmer too. I guess he can't help himself, the way they throw themselves at him. Maybe he'll settle down someday, but I doubt it."

Contessa still heard her laughing as she went back in the house to resume her cleaning.

Rick had woken early and driven over to Juliana Airport. He had ordered a crate of pineapples, and the last time one arrived, the airport staff left it sitting half the day in the hot sun so that most of the fruit had spoiled. This time he was going to pick it up himself. His guests loved fresh pineapple mixed with papaya for breakfast. As he crossed the tarmac, he saw that the plane from Puerto Rico had already landed. Great timing, he thought. He'd be able to load the fruit right onto the truck.

Passengers were walking toward the terminal, most of them dressed in white suits and tropical prints. One passenger stood out from the others. He was pale-skinned and dressed in a conservative dark suit. Rick paused and stiffened in disbelief. He started to turn away, but the man had already recognized him.

"Rick!" he called. "Great to see you. How did you

know I'd be coming in today? I thought I'd surprise everybody."

Rick took the offered hand. "Oh, you certainly surprised everybody all right," he said. "Welcome home, Robert."

CHAPTER 10

W ill Philips crammed the last of his clothing into his duffel bag. It was finally over. He was out of school for good. He knew he'd learned a little about plant diseases and increasing yields, but apart from those things, the last four years had been a total waste of time. True, he had loved the glory of playing basketball. He had experienced the thrill of coming out onto the court before screaming fans and the thrill of walking off again, sweaty and exhausted but triumphant. But that was kid stuff and he wasn't sad that it was over. It hadn't even occurred to him to say yes to the scout who wanted him to try out for a professional team. That would have meant staying in the States, and Will was sure he didn't want to do that. He had enough of America. The rest of the world was waiting to be explored.

He planned to go home briefly, because he was sure his father expected it. He had been amazed when Robert had just taken off for Europe without coming home. Will had received Robert's first postcard from London: "I decided to take a break for a while," Robert had written. "I'm seeing the world before I put my nose to father's grindstone. P.S. Don't tell Dad where I am."

The postcard had been completely unlike Robert. Robert was usually the one who planned things in detail. He never did anything on the spur of the moment. Heading for Europe on a whim was so unusual for Robert, it gave Will the courage to do the same thing.

The next postcard had been from Paris. "Europe is great but lonesome. Why don't you join me? I've met some people who are traveling by bus to Katmandu. What do you think?"

Will thought it sounded like a great idea. He'd love to trek through the Himalayas and take a boat down the Ganges . He'd come home with enough adventures and experience to last him a lifetime. He stuffed the postcards into his duffel bag and slung it onto his back. He was really looking forward to the summer.

"Marigot? Where is that child?" Madame de Gaulle demanded. She swept through the living room to find Marigot staring out the window.

"I thought I asked you to put flowers on the dining table," Marigot's mother said angrily. "Mr. Christof's guests will be arriving in a few minutes. And then I need you to take out the langoustines for the first course. I've made my special spicy mayonnaise sauce for them." She paused. "Marigot, are you listening to me?" she demanded.

Marigot took one look at her mother and ran from the room. Madame de Gaulle followed her. "What's the matter with you, child?" she demanded.

"Nothing," Marigot said shortly. "Nothing's the matter with me."

"You've been acting very strangely," Madame de Gaulle

commented. "You left in the middle of dinner last night and tonight you're in another world. I might get the impression that you thought domestic work was below somebody who'd been educated in the convent."

"Oh, no, *Maman*," Marigot said. "I don't mind helping you, honestly. It's just that I'm not feeling too well. The heat seems so oppressive here. I've been feeling so dizzy and tired lately. "Madame de Gaulle's gaze sharpened. "Is there something you'd like to tell me?" she demanded.

"No, nothing." Marigot turned away.

Madame de Gaulle put a thin, bony hand on her daughter's shoulder. "You can't just ignore it and pretend it will go away, you know."

"I don't know what you're talking about." Marigot tossed her head defiantly.

"I think you do," Madame de Gaulle said more gently now. "You think I'm blind, child? I've been pregnant myself, you know. I know the signs."

Marigot turned huge, imploring eyes on her mother. "Oh, *Maman*, what am I going to do?" she said.

"Is it Mr. Will's son?" she asked.

Marigot nodded.

"That's all right, then," Madame de Gaulle said. "He'll soon be home from school and he'll have to do the right thing, won't he?"

"But *Maman*, what if won't marry me? I'm only an islander after all …."

Madame de Gaulle's slap across the face made her daughter recoil in shock. "Don't let me ever hear you talk like that again, child," she said. "You're as good as anybody on this island. If I was good enough to share the life of the greatest Frenchman of this century and make him happy, then you're a fit wife for this young man. Don't ever think that because your skin is darker than theirs you don't have all the qualities, all the intelligence that they have. You are a lady. Good enough for the best and definitely good enough for Mr. Will." She stopped and took her daughter's face in her hands. "You do love him, don't you?"

"I love him so much it hurts, *Maman*," Marigot whispered.

"That's all I needed to know," Madame de Gaulle said. "I'll speak to Mr. Christof after dinner tonight. He's a gentleman. He'll make sure his son does the right thing by you."

Robert Philips stood on the Rialto Bridge in Venice and watched the gondolas pass beneath him. All around him the city exploded with beauty. Stallkeepers hawked glass beads and leather goods from their little booths along the bridge, tourists passed him, smiling and laughing. Everybody looked relaxed and happy except for him.

"It's no use," he said to himself. "I've tried to run away and it's no use. I take my misery with me wherever I go." He felt so completely alone in the middle of this crowd. Nothing seemed to matter anymore now that his Contessa was gone. Thinking of her name sent a stab of pain through his heart. The only thing left for him to do was to go home and get on with his life. Responsibilities awaited him. His father wanted to hand the export side of the business over to him right away. Maybe if he worked hard enough and long enough, he wouldn't have the time to think anymore …. He headed back to his hotel and booked the next flight out of town.

He arrived two days later on a small plane out of Puerto Rico. For the first time in many months, Robert felt happy. He couldn't wait to be home with his father and island friends. He caught a glimpse of Trade Winds. It would be great to see Rick and Will again. Maybe they'd take the boat out and go spear fishing like they used to. Suddenly it felt good to be alive again.

As he stepped out of the plane into blinding sunshine, the first person he saw was Rick. It occurred to him that Rick had somehow gotten word of his arrival and come to meet him. He hurried toward his old friend, his hand extended.

"So how about it, Rick," he said. "Can you give me a ride back to Plantation House? I'd rather ride with you than take a taxi."

He thought Rick looked doubtful for a moment, then he said, "Sure Robert. No problem. I just have to pick up a crate of pineapple, then we'll go."

Soon they were bouncing along country roads.

"So how are things at Trade Winds?" Robert asked. "Busy?"

"Hanging in there," Rick said. "There are still so many improvements that need to be made, but business is starting to pick up."

"That's good," Robert said. "You've worked so hard to make a go of that place. I hope Paradise Rum is still standing."

"It was yesterday."

"That's great. And my father. How is he?"

"He's fine. Worried about you. Nobody knew where you were."

"I know. I felt guilty about that, but I just couldn't come straight home from school and face everybody. I needed time to myself."

"Time to find yourself?"

"Time to get over a woman," Robert said. "I met a woman, Rick. An incredible woman. I know it sounds corny, but it was love at first sight for both of us. I never thought that kind of love really existed...."He gave an embarrassed little laugh, then cleared his throat. "What's the sense in talking about it. It only brings back painful memories."

"She left you?" Rick asked, although he knew the answer. It was killing him to hear Robert's story, but he wanted to hear his version.

"She had a brute of a husband, but she decided to stay with him after all." He gave a huge sigh. "I'll never understand women," he said. "I could have sworn ... I was moving heaven and earth to get her away from him. I had this lawyer who would have handled the Mexican divorce ... and then I got a cold little letter. Nothing more."

Rick swallowed hard. "How do you know her husband didn't force her to write the letter?" he said.

"Please. I've thought of that a thousand times. But why wouldn't she try to get word to me somehow?" Robert's voice trembled as he spoke.

"Maybe he was holding her son hostage?"

Robert looked at him sharply. "How did you know about her son? I never mentioned a son."

"Because she's staying at Trade Winds right now," Rick said.

"Contessa's at Trade Winds? Here? On the island?"

"That's right. She came looking for you, but you weren't here. I let her use one of my bungalows …." Rick had to steady his hands on the wheel of the car. It physically hurt him to tell Robert where Contessa was.

Robert was beside himself with excitement. "I can't believe it. She's here and she's fine and her husband hasn't been bothering her?"

"Her husband is dead. Killed in a Mafia shootout."

Robert grasped Rick's shoulder, almost making the car swerve off the road. "Rick, do you know what this means? We can be married right away. Oh, God, it's incredible. It's a miracle , Rick. I'm going to have you as my best man … can you take me to her now? I can't wait to see her face when she sees me get out of the car."

"Neither can I," Rick said.

Contessa walked alone on the shore. It was just after sunset. Twilight had come on suddenly, as it does in the tropics, and lights twinkled from boats making their way into port. She had just returned from a big party at Robert's house, a party given in her honor to announce their approaching marriage. She had met so many people, all wanting to know everything about her, and now she just wanted to be alone.

Since Rick's car had pulled up in front of the hotel and Robert, not Rick, had stepped out, she had been in a state of turmoil. Everything had happened so fast, she felt as if she had been running on a treadmill. She wasn't unhappy, but she needed to get her thoughts in order, especially her thoughts about Rick. With her marriage only a few days away, she had to be sure she was making the right decision.

Robert had taken it for granted that they would be married immediately. "We can't have you living in that shack any longer," he had said. "We must get more suitable quarters fixed up for you at the big house. We can plan the wedding together from there."

He hadn't questioned whether she'd still want to marry him. His own love for her hadn't wavered one bit, and he expected her to feel the same way about him. And in many ways she did. It was wonderful to be so completely loved by a man, to see him looking at her with such adoration. She knew in her heart that this was a man who would never let her down, who would treat her like a princess all her life. And yet she also knew that close by there was another man who could set her on fire.

She kicked off her shoes and walked along the edge of the ocean, feeling the cool water wash over her toes. She was sure she would have a good life with Robert. His family owned half the island. He had a steady job and a bright future. She wasn't completely sure her new father-in-law liked her, but he had welcomed her to the family.

"If you can keep my son here, in one place, and get him to settle down and start working, then that's the most important thing," Christof said to her. "One day he'll have to take over Paradise Rum. That's what all his business degrees are for. He is going to make our already prosperous enterprise even more profitable."

"I'm sure anything Robert put his hand to would prosper," she said simply.

Christof had nodded. He seemed to approve of her answer. She was a little scared of Christof though. He looked at her as if he could read her every thought. *You're not really good enough for my son,* his look said. She wondered what it would be like living in the same house as him.

"Why can't we get our own place?" she had asked Robert.

"We will in time," Robert said. "It doesn't make any sense right now. There are all those empty rooms at the big house. And my father all alone. You must be patient, darling. When I have Paradise Rum running the way I intend, I'll build you your dream house, I promise."

She raised her face for him to kiss. "You're very good to me, Robert," she said.

He brushed her forehead with his lips. "I intend to spoil you mercilessly for the rest of your life," he said. "It was a miracle that we found each other again, and I don't ever intend to let you go."

She had hardly seen Rick since Robert's arrival. She really had no idea how he had taken the news. He had brought Robert to see her, so he couldn't have been too upset. She tried to tell herself that Rick was interested only in her body. They had made fabulous love together, but that was hardly the basis for a lifetime of happiness. And he had never suggested a long-term relationship. Perhaps what Aimee had said was true. Maybe he was the sort of man who got tired of women quickly and moved on to newer and greener pastures. Maybe their whirlwind passion would have spent itself in a few weeks, and she would have had the humiliation of knowing that he was involved with someone else. Telling herself this made things much easier. Soon enough, Rick would be a happy memory rather than a painful reminder of her indecision.

She had Joey to think of too: Rick owned a hotel with more liabilities than assets. He might never make a go of it. But Robert would provide well for her and her child. She must choose security for Joey's sake as well as her own. She remembered what it had been like to be down to her last few dollars, not knowing what was going to happen to her next. She never wanted to feel like that again. And perhaps Robert would awake in her the same passion that Rick had. She looked forward to being with Robert. He was still behaving like the perfect gentleman toward her. He had kissed her and held her close, but anything more had to wait until after the wedding. "I want you to know that I respect you completely," he had said as he escorted her back to her own quarters.

She leaned over to pick up a shell, and as she straightened, she saw a figure in white coming down the steps to the beach. Through the falling darkness she recognized Rick's easy, graceful movement.

"I thought I might find you here," he said. He came to join her at the water's edge. "Robert's family and friends can be a little overwhelming."

"Very overwhelming," she said. "I was introduced to hundreds of people and I've forgotten all their names."

She turned toward him, and they stood looking at each other for the first time in days.

"So," he said, clearing his throat. "You're really going to marry Robert?"

"It seems that way."

"Is that what you really want?"

"Yes," she said. "It's what I really want."

"I see." He turned and stared out at the sea, his arms folded across his chest. Contessa rested her hand lightly on his arm. "What we had, Rick, it was only physical, wasn't it? It was great, but it was just physical attraction." She paused, waiting for him to agree. "You can't build a life on that basis. I have to do what I think is best for myself and my son," she continued.

"You know I worship Joey," he said in a strangled voice. "I would have been a great father to him. And I worship you too, Contessa."

"You'd soon tire of me," she said, attempting to laugh. "I've heard you never keep a girlfriend for more than a month."

"It would have been different with you," he whispered. "I didn't want to fall in love with you, Contessa. It just happened. I think you fell in love with me too, only you won't admit it."

"Stop saying things like that, Rick. I'm doing this for both of us," she said unconvincingly. "I've made up my mind to marry Robert, and I can't go back on my word now. The wedding's all planned. The whole island's invited."

"That's hardly a reason to get married to someone for the rest of your life," Rick said dryly. "Love should enter into it, Contessa."

"He adores me. He'll give me a good life." Her grip tightened on his arm. "I want you to forget all about me, Rick, just like I'm going to try to forget all about you. I want you to come to my wedding and wish me happiness."

"I wish you happiness, Contessa, but don't ask me to come to your wedding," he said. Abruptly he shook himself loose from her grip and ran down the beach, disappearing into the darkness.

CHAPTER 11

W ill Philips eased his large frame out of the taxi and stood looking at Plantation House with satisfaction. It was good to be home, knowing that he'd never have to go back to school in America again. He had a diploma in his duffel which would make his father happy, and now he was ready to start enjoying life. He'd stick around for a couple of weeks, long enough to see Marigot again, and then he was heading over to Europe. He was annoyed that Robert had backed out of the Nepal trip, but then, he never expected Robert to do something like that in the first place. But that wasn't going to stop Will from seeing the world. Even if he took a year or so off to travel around, he'd come back older and wiser and ready to devote the rest of his life to Paradise Rum.

He slung his duffel bag over his shoulder and sprinted up the steps into the house. As if by magic, Madame de Gaulle appeared, her arms full of flowers.

"Dante? I need more orchids," she called. "The arrangement on the back veranda looks kind of bare … ." She stopped, noticing Will in the doorway. "So?" she said. "You decided to come home."

"Hello, Madame de Gaulle," Will said with his usual

friendly grin. "Anyone miss me? "

"Not that you'd notice," she said calmly.

"What's with the flowers? What's going on?"

"Your brother's wedding," she said. "Your father was afraid you were going miss it."

"Robert's getting married?" Will couldn't have been more surprised." "Last time I heard from him he was in Venice, and now he's getting married."

"He's found the lady he thought he lost," Madame de Gaulle said, "and now he's going to do the right thing and marry her. He's ready to take responsibility and be a man."

"Well, hooray for Robert," Will said sarcastically. "He always was the responsible type."

"We expected you to arrive some time ago," Madame de Gaulle said accusingly. "You've been out of school for a month. Your father was trying to contact you."

"Yeah," Will said, "but I stopped off to visit friends on the way home. One of them has a ranch in Wyoming and he was planning to drive cattle, so I thought I'd give it a try. It was kind of fun—real dusty, sore seat, but fun."

He could sense Madame de Gaulle's disapproving stare and cleared his throat. "Where's the old man? I better go pay my respects. You know, the prodigal son returns!" Will laughed at the thought.

"He's in his study," Madame de Gaulle said, "going over the guest list, I think."

"I'll surprise him," Will said.

Madame de Gaulle raised an eyebrow. "I think maybe that he'll surprise you," she said.

The wedding took place on the spectacular veranda of

the Plantation House. The Chief justice on the Dutch side of the island married them. He was a great friend of Christof's and included happy remembrances of Robert's childhood throughout the ceremony.

As Robert watched her coming up the aisle to join him, Joey in a white shirt and linen shorts walking ahead as ring bearer, he felt that his heart would burst with pride and happiness. What had he done in his life to earn the honor of marrying the most beautiful woman on earth? She looked radiant in her long gown and wide-brimmed hat. He stepped up proudly to take her hand, and she looked at him shyly.

Contessa realized that she was holding her breath all the way down the aisle. I hope I can get through this without fainting, she thought. The little church seemed to be stifling. The smell of incense hovered in the thick air and made her head spin. She felt very far away and unreal as she answered the questions the priest asked her and crossed herself for the final blessing.

Only a few people had been invited to the ceremony itself, The island churches were not built for vast crowds. But there were hundreds at the reception, spilling onto the verandas and over the lawns. On an island the size of St. Martin you took care not to leave anyone out of an invitation—it didn't do to make enemies. Plantation workers had been turned into waiters and waitresses for the day, moving among the crowd with trays of crab claws, shrimp, and champagne, and Philips rum drinks. Robert and Contessa wandered among them, both moving together as if in a dream. He still couldn't believe that the beautiful woman on his arm now belonged to him. He noticed the admiring glances from the other men as he accepted the handshakes and congratulations. His eyes scanned the crowd for those most important to him.

"I can't believe Rick didn't show," he said. "It's so odd. He knew I wanted him to stand up for us. I hope it's nothing serious. Something must have come up at the hotel."

Contessa looked at him and nodded. She didn't want her voice to give anything away. If she had seen Rick before the ceremony, she was sure she would have turned and run to him. What have I done? she asked herself. She turned to sneak a glance at Robert's handsome, serious face. I do love him, she mused. We'll have a good life together. So why did she hope against hope that Rick would have changed his mind and come to her wedding after all?

Will had been looking for Marigot and found her at last in the kitchen.

"What are you doing in here?" he asked. "You're not supposed to be working. Everyone's getting ready to sit down, and I want you out there with me."

Marigot turned away, pretending to be occupied with the food. "I'd rather not," she said.

"But Marigot!" Will pleaded. "I thought we agreed we'd announce it today? I can't say anything if you're not there, can I?"

She turned to him with pleading eyes. "Go ahead and announce it if you like, but I'd rather stay out of sight. I don't want to cause embarrassment."

Will walked over and put his arms around her. "They're

all going to have to get used to it," he said tenderly.

"Please, Will, don't make me," she said.

"Of course I'd never make you do anything you don't want," he said. "But I think you'll be surprised. Most people will be delighted, except for a few old squares. And we don't care what they think."

He looked up as servants came hurrying in to pick up trays of food. "I guess I'd better get out there," he said.

As he came out, guests were being ushered to the long white tables set up in the shade, and a full banquet was served. Christof gave a speech. The couple was toasted. Then Will rose to his feet. "First I want to congratulate my brother on having picked such a stunningly beautiful bride. I don't know what she sees in him ... but I know they'll be very happy together." Will grinned as everyone had a good laugh.

"And now I have some news of my own, and this seems the right occasion to make it public. Whatever got into Robert seems to be catching. I've decided to follow his example and get married too."

There was an expectant ripple of conversation around the table. "I have asked Mademoiselle Marigot de Gaulle to do me the honor of becoming my wife and she has accepted. We plan to be married very soon."

He swallowed hard and sat down to what he expected would be mixed reaction. Some people were already thumping him on the back and telling him he was a lucky devil, but he could sense others looking at him with disgust, as if he had let his race down by choosing to marry an island native. Robert's face was one of the latter, but he retained his composure and continued drinking toasts, laughing and talking until dessert had been eaten and guests were saying their good-byes. Contessa went inside to change out of her wedding dress and Will found himself alone with Robert and Christof.

"How could you!" Robert blurted out. "How could you cheapen my wedding day with an announcement like that. What on earth has gotten into you? What makes you think you can bring a native into the family?"

"I am going to marry what you call a native, Robert, and with Father's blessing," Will said.

Robert spun around to face his father. "You approve of this? Your son marrying the servant's daughter?"

Christof shifted uneasily. "She's not exactly a servant, is she? She's above that. She's almost family. And Marigot's an educated girl."

"Marigot's also a black girl," Robert said. "Do you want those mixed grandchildren running around Plantation House?"

Christof sighed and put a big hand on his son's shoulder. "You and I will never think alike, Robert," he said. "It's funny, but a lot of the things you say were things that made me leave my own country. The Germany I escaped from was full of the kind of people you think are so superior, and yet they were behaving more like savages than any island native. Will and Marigot's marriage symbolizes for me the best of this island and what I like most about it. I see it as an example for the rest of the world. If we can all get along in harmony here, then there's hope."

Robert glared at his brother. "I assume that she's pregnant. I can't see any other reason for your rushing into marriage. Are you sure it's yours?"

"You creep!" Will said angrily.

"I just hope you're not considering living in Father's house. It would be most unfair to make Contessa have to treat Marigot like an equal."

"You're right," Will said. "After all, Marigot is an educated, intelligent woman. Not a cheap tart with dollar signs in her eyes."

Robert's hand clenched into a fist. "You take that back immediately!" he roared.

Christof sprang between them, his superior strength holding the young men apart. "Stop it right now or I'll knock both your heads together the way I used to when you were children," he threatened. "Now, listen to me, and listen good," he said as he released them. "Plantation House belongs to me. Anyone who lives in it does so by my invitation only, and obeys my rules. If you cannot all get along, find a place of your own to live. I will not tolerate malice or disrespect under my roof. Do I make myself clear?"

"Yes, Father," both men said in unison.

"Good. Now shake hands with each other. Go on," he instructed them. Unwillingly, both men extended their hands. "Now," Christof went on, "you've both chosen brides for yourself. I hope you understand that this means you're not boys anymore. You're men with adult responsibilities. You're also my employees. I expect hard work and dedication to the company from both of you, in which case someday you and your heirs will own it … or I'll fire you and disinherit you. Understand."

"Yes, Father," Robert murmured. Will nodded.

"Now, get out there and thank your guests for coming," Christof said.

Up in her new bedroom Contessa attempted to take off her wedding dress. She was hot and tired and all she wanted to do was to get away with Robert to the hideaway in St. Lucia where they were going to spend their honeymoon. There was a light tap on her door and she looked up. Marigot was standing there.

"I wondered if you wanted some help," she said hesitantly, "seeing that we're about to be sisters-in-law."

Contessa had never felt at ease around Marigot or her mother. In her former attempts to talk to them, she had found them haughty and aloof. But at this moment Contessa felt very much in need of sisterly attention. She also noticed that for once Marigot was looking very unsure of herself. This afternoon's celebration couldn't have been easy for her either.

"Of course, come on in," Contessa said, holding out her hand to Marigot. "I'm having a problem with this stupid wedding dress. Why do they always make zippers at the back?"

"Maybe to give husbands some practice for undressing their wives?" Marigot said with a light laugh. She unzipped the dress for her and helped her step out of it. "You have a lovely figure," she said admiringly.

"So do you," Contessa said.

Marigot shook her head. "Not anymore," she said, and held the caftan she was wearing tight across her belly. "I can't believe how quickly I'm growing. Christof suggested a double wedding, but I didn't want all those people to see me like this."

She held out a green silk dress for Contessa to step into.

"That's why you hid away," Contessa said. "Everyone was asking Will where you were. They wanted to congratulate you."

"Not all of them, I'm sure," Marigot said.

"Most of them," Contessa said.

Marigot looked away. "It's not going to be easy for Will or the baby," she said. "This is a small island, and there's still too much prejudice among both blacks and whites."

Contessa patted her arm. "Christof makes it clear that he's given his blessing, and that's all that matters really," she said.

Marigot gave her a dazzling smile. "Thank you, Contessa," she said. "To tell you the truth, I was worried about what you'd think of me and how I'd fit in here. I'm glad you turned out to be supportive. It makes it so much easier. And who knows, it might be fun—you and Robert will have babies too and they'll all grow up together in this house."

She went over and gave Contessa a kiss on her cheek, then she slipped out of the room again. Contessa stood looking thoughtfully out of the window. Down below she could see Robert surrounded by friends, shaking hands and acting like the proud groom. She wondered if Marigot might possess some of her mother's power and intuition. Did she sense the truth when she spoke about babies playing together in the house? Contessa felt dizzy and had to sit down. Maybe it wasn't true after all. She'd read that women's cycles could become irregular in the presence of stress or upheaval. Maybe that's what it was. All the trauma of the past few weeks could play havoc with any woman's monthly cycle. She couldn't be absolutely certain that she was pregnant with Rick Sommers's child.

Will and Marigot were married two weeks later at an event that in no way resembled his brother's lavish wedding. Only Marigot's relatives plus Will's father and a few of his friends, including Rick, were present at a ceremony that took place on the back lawn between the big house and Madame de Gaulle's cottage. A Dominican missionary monk officiated. It was a brief ceremony with a Catholic blessing, followed immediately by the sort of celebration found only in the Caribbean. A steel band appeared, together with various drums. Shoes were discarded and soon everyone, black and white, was dancing to the throbbing beat.

"Are you sure you should be doing this?" Will asked Marigot, who was flinging herself around with abandon.

"Of course," she said.

"It won't harm the baby?"

"No, and neither will anything else you might have in mind," she said, slinking up to him seductively and wrapping her arms around his neck while her body still swayed to the rhythm of the drums.

"When can we slip away?" Will whispered in her ear.

She laughed. "Don't be so impatient. I want to dance awhile with my guests. I promise I'll make it up to you later," she added, giving him a smoldering look over her shoulder as she moved away.

Will's pulse quickened. At this moment he was very, very glad he had come home to St. Martin.

CHAPTER 12

Rick Sommers sat alone in the lobby of his hotel and stared out at the blue sea beyond. The piece of paper he held in his hand fluttered in the sea breeze. He sat motionless for some time, then he gave a long, heartfelt sigh and got to his feet. So much to be done and he didn't know where to start. He glanced down at the paper. It was a check for thirty thousand dollars, the total amount the insurance company had awarded him for the death of his parents. Thirty thousand dollars to pay for the loss of the two most important people in your life! It was hardly just. In fact, it was almost insulting. He was inclined to send the check back to them, to tell them what they could do with their lousy insurance policy.

Then he reminded himself that at least now he could start on some of the improvements he'd been talking about. A new roof was out of the question, of course. That would cost much more than thirty thousand, but there was a host of other things: better furniture for the main entrance hall, refurbishing the rooms, repainting the out-side of the hotel … and now that he had the money to begin, he didn't think he had the energy. He sighed again. Since Contessa had left to marry Robert, nothing seemed to matter anymore. He couldn't believe that he, Rick Sommers, noted playboy of St. Martin since he was sixteen, could have fallen so heavily for one woman. He hadn't meant to. God, how he'd tried to keep away from her and do the right thing by Robert, but it had happened all the same. And he not only missed Contessa, but little Joey as well. He'd fallen for that kid in a big way. He had found it easy to picture himself teaching the kid how to fish and steer the boat and dive. He imagined Joey looking up at him with those big, solemn eyes and calling him Daddy.

Rick tried to stop the tears from welling up in his eyes. Christ, he never knew he was so soft. Imagine crying over some damned woman. He must pull himself together—get on with his life. She'd made her choice and she'd chosen security and money over love and happiness. She'd be sorry in the end, he thought. He bet Robert Philips didn't know how to satisfy a woman, not like he could. Give her a few months and she'll be begging for me, he decided.

In the meantime he'd prove to her he didn't care. He'd pick up his old life, the good times he had before he was saddled with the hotel. He'd start hanging out at the clubs again and he'd work his way through all the desirable women on the island!

He stuffed the check into his pocket and returned to his bungalow to change into clean white pants and a crisp white shirt. He'd go down to the casino. That was a great place to pick up beautiful women. And right now he didn't care who they were as long as they were hot and willing in bed.

Rick jumped into his mini-Moke and headed down to a casino in Philipsburg over on the Dutch side where gambling was allowed. There was a good-size crowd around the tables as he walked in and he ran his eyes appreciatively over several pairs of legs. Definitely enough talent for one evening. God, it had been so long, he'd almost forgotten how! He bought a hundred dollars worth of chips and stationed himself at the roulette table beside an attractive dark girl, rather French-looking, but with that unmistakable hint of the islands about her.

"What's a good number?" he asked.

She looked up in surprise, then let her gaze travel over him, obviously liking what she saw. "Two," she said. "Two is a good number tonight." She had an attractive French-Caribbean accent.

"Very well, two it is," Rick said, and placed two ten-dollar chips on the two.

The roulette wheel spun and landed on fifteen.

"I'm sorry," the young woman said. "Maybe two is a good number for other things. I tell you what, you can choose the number for me this time and we'll be even."

"Okay," he said. "Twenty-five."

"Why twenty-five?" she asked. "Is that your age?"

"Close enough," he said. He wasn't going to admit to being just out of college.

"Good choice, mine too," she said. "You must be a mind reader." She took five ten-dollar chips and put them on twenty-five. The wheel spun. *"Vingt-cinq,"* the croupier called, and pushed a large pile of chips in the direction of the young woman.

"You're bringing me luck," she said. "I'm Monique."

"Rick."

"Here's your half, then, Rick." She pushed some of the chips across to him.

"That's okay. Keep them," Rick said. "I know another way you can pay me back."

"Wicked," she said, giving him a throaty laugh. "Are you staying around here?"

"No, I own a hotel over at Oyster Pond."

"You own it?"

"Yes, Trade Winds. You must have heard of it. Big white place on the ocean."

"Can't say that I have," she said, "but I'm willing to get a guided tour from the owner, especially if the tour includes the private accommodations."

She closed her eyes and ran her tongue over her lips. Rick suddenly wanted to laugh. It was all so easy and so predictable. He could pick up any woman he wanted, anytime. A wave of distaste came over him. Did he want this one, he wondered. He let his gaze sweep around the room to see if there was anyone he'd prefer to make a play for before he took off in his car with Monique. Suddenly he found himself staring into the cool, patrician face of Grace Nobel.

"Well, hi there," she said. "Just the man I've been wanting to see."

"Don't tell me you got amoebic dysentery from the ice in the drink you had at my hotel and you've brought your lawyer to sue."

She flushed. "Look, I meant to apologize about that," she said. "I was very rude to you that day and I've been feeling bad about it ever since."

"Not bad enough to ride over and apologize in person," he said.

"You were partly to blame. You let me go on making a fool of myself."

"It wasn't hard," Rick said.

A spasm of anger crossed Grace's face, then she forced herself to relax and smile. "Do you think we could forget about old quarrels, Mr. Sommers, and start over. If we're going to be neighbors on the same small island, it's better to get along, isn't it? Couldn't we pretend our first meeting never happened?"

"If you want to," Rick said. "It's all the same to me. One cranky woman can't ruin my day."

She frowned again, then composed her face. She had business to get to. "I have been meaning to pay you a visit."

"I'm sure our lunches still don't measure up to your standard," Rick said, "not if you're bringing Mr. Vanderwhatsit."

"Mr. Vanderwhatsit died," Grace said simply.

"I'm sorry."

"Thank you. I'm getting used to it. I'm learning to make my own life."

He nodded. "I know how you feel," he said.

She looked around the room. "Do you think we could go somewhere to talk," she said. "I've been meaning to come over because I've a business proposition that I'd like to discuss with you."

A flicker of amusement crossed Rick's face. "What kind of proposition?"

"Not the kind you'd get from most of the women here," she said.

As if on cue, Monique slid an arm through Rick's. *"Chéri,* I'm bored," she said. "And I've lost all my money. Why don't you give me that tour of your hotel now?"

"Uh … later, Monique," Rick said. "I have to talk business with an old friend."

He motioned to Grace, and they moved away. Monique looked surprised and annoyed. She made an indignant little noise and turned her back on them.

"I hope I haven't spoiled anything," she said, glancing back at the pouting girl. "I could always come over to discuss this in the morning."

Rick shook his head. "It's all right. I'd known her for only ten minutes and I was already bored with her. I think I'm losing interest in the one-night stand. I must be getting old."

Grace laughed. "Burned out at twenty-one? That's funny."

They stepped out into the balmy night air. Lights twinkled along the waterfront.

"How did you know how old I was?" Rick asked.

"I do my homework," she said. "I know quite a lot about you, Mr. Rick Sommers."

"Like what?"

"Like that hotel of yours is teetering on the brink of disaster."

"Not anymore. We're doing just fine now."

"Fine if the weather holds up. But you could be doing fabulously. You have one of the best sites on the island. You should be full almost year round with a waiting list."

"It's not all that easy. You have to build up a clientele. We'd just gotten ourselves going when the last hurricane brought us all that bad publicity."

"You need to advertise, get some positive PR. How else is anyone in the States going to know about you?"

Rick shrugged. "I wouldn't know where to start," he said.

"That's where I come in," Grace said.

"You?"

"Yes. When I came to your hotel that day I came because it looked like a place for rich people. Then I got inside and I saw the furniture and the peeling paint and I was disappointed. If you want the hotel to do well, you must turn it into the sort of place rich people expect. I know what rich people like. I was around them long enough to know exactly what they expect from a hotel."

"What are you suggesting?"

"That I start working with you. I have friends and connections with the know-how and the style to make Trade Winds into the resort of the French Caribbean. I know where to advertise, how to furnish, what sort of staff to hire ...." Grace wasn't bragging. She was just honest. And a job like this would mean being able to stay in St. Martin.

"That costs a lot of money, to say nothing of your salary," Rick reminded her.

"It can cost a lot less than you think," she said. "Of course you'll have to put up some money. But I'll work for nothing to begin with."

Rick looked at her suspiciously. "And what's in it for you?"

"Something to do with myself," she said. "I've always been a working girl. I used to be an airline stewardess until I met Andrew. I'm not used to being idle. I suppose I could go back to my old job, but I've come to like it here. This job would be perfect for me. It would give me a challenge and it's something I know I can do well."

Rick looked at her standing there, her elegant dark hair blowing in the wind. "What have I got to lose?" he asked her.

And she smiled.

"You did what?" Rick demanded.

Grace eyed him coolly. "You can see for yourself. I decided to double your prices."

"Are you out of your mind?" he shrieked. "Who the hell gave you permission to place that ad in the first place and then to make up your own prices?"

She frowned. "Don't swear. It lowers the tone of the place."

He glared at her. "Lady, you ain't heard nothing yet. Don't make me use the rest of my vocabulary."

She shrugged and turned away from him. "I can't see what you're so upset about. You gave me carte blanche to give the hotel what it needed ...."

"Yeah, I meant flowers and furniture—stuff like that. Not full-page ads and price hikes! Grace, I can't fill the hotel at fifty dollars a night, and you advertise it at hundred? What are you trying to do, bankrupt me?"

She still remained calm. "Trust me," she said. "I know what I'm doing and I know what a certain type of person would expect to pay for a hotel like this. You have to understand the psychology of the rich, Rick. They want to go to a place that they know other people can't afford. It gives them pleasure just knowing that the masses will never be able to stay there. Rich people are all snobs. You have to play on snob value."

"Which was why you put a full-page ad in this magazine?" He waved the glossy publication in her face.

"Of course. It attracts the right people."

"I hope you're right," he snapped, because that's a hell of a lot of money to waste on an ad and we're going to look pretty damned stupid if the guests we have stop coming because they can't afford us anymore."

She looked around the foyer. "You have to admit what I've done so far has made a difference. The guests certainly seem to appreciate all the little things like fresh flowers in their rooms and on their breakfast trays. The menus have improved."

"Okay, fine, those things are good," Rick said, "and we grow the flowers in the garden, so they don't cost money."

"Must you always be so damned money conscious?"

"Maybe it's because I watched my parents struggle to get this place going and we've never had enough of the stuff," Rick said bitterly. "I'd hate to lose it all now on some stupid gamble to attract the rich and shut out the rest of the world."

She eyed him with confidence. "You have to know what you want, then go for it."

He stood facing her. "You're so sure of yourself, aren't you?"

"Yes, I am," she said. "You trusted me on the menus and the decorations; now trust me on this."

He flung down the magazine. "It seems like I have no choice," he said. "This issue is already in the most exclusive homes in the States."

The phone rang at the front desk. Grace sprinted across to answer it. "Trade Winds," she said in her low, smooth voice. "Party of four for next Wednesday ... oh, I'm sorry, we're fully booked for that date." Rick spluttered and tried to get the phone away from her, but she successfully turned her back on him. "No, wait a minute, you're in luck. I see we had a cancellation this morning. It seems the United Nations is going into emergency session so the ambassador couldn't make it after all. What name was that, please?"

She put the phone down with a satisfied smile. "Wouldn't work, eh? That was Mr. and Mrs. DuPont of Palm Beach with their friends the Whitneys. She read about us at the beauty parlor in her favorite magazine."

She started pacing up and down. "God, I hope the food will be good enough for them. I really think we should start upgrading the staff, Rick."

"What's wrong with Aimee's cooking?"

"Nothing if you like simple island fare and you don't mind waiting while she shuffles around that kitchen at zero miles an hour. The jet set wants a well-known international chef. I have heard through the grapevine that Monsieur Antoine who is currently on Martinique at Villa Ritz isn't happy there. If we could get him ..."

"At what sort of price?"

"Oh, he won't come cheap, but his fans will follow him here."

"And what am I going to do with Aimee?"

Grace shrugged again. "She does simple things quite well. Have her work under him—just don't let her clean the rooms. She's terribly lazy and she sweeps the dirt under the rugs."

Rick had to laugh. "Why did I ever agree to this crazy idea in the first place?" he asked.

"Because you knew I had what it takes," she said, "and because I'm a beautiful woman and you never could resist beautiful women."

Rick watched her walk away. She was right, he thought with surprise. She is a very beautiful woman. So why hadn't he reacted as he usually did when a beautiful woman was close to him? Was she doing something that turned him off? He decided that the first encounter with Grace had made him forever wary. If there was one thing he hated, it was being put down by a woman … and if there was another, it was being rejected by one. And he'd had his fill of both recently.

Almost every day he ran into Contessa somewhere on the island. She was clearly enjoying her new role as First Lady of Paradise Rum. He had seen her shopping in town, striding back to the car while the chauffeur followed, hard-ly able to see over a mountain of purchases. He had seen her dining with Robert at the best restaurants on the French side, always stunningly dressed, always talking a little too loudly. And each time he had shrunk back into the shadows so that they didn't have to meet. He was so scared she might already have forgotten who he was!

"Damn women," he said out loud. At least he'd make sure that the relationship with Grace stayed strictly business, because the more he looked at her, the more he decided that he could very easily be attracted to her. She didn't have

Contessa's flamboyant beauty and sensuality, but she certainly had style. Rick sighed. It was no use thinking about her. Grace thought of him as a womanizer, and maybe she was right! He did like beautiful women. He found it hard to stay away from them. He decided to go down to the new Coq d'Or nightclub again. At least the girls he met there didn't want to dominate or humiliate him. In fact they were grateful for the least little bit of attention he paid them.

As the weeks went by, Rick had to admit grudgingly that Grace had been right about everything. M. Antoine took up residence in the kitchen and guests promptly arrived to try his cuisine. The ads in *Town and Country* were followed by similar ads in *The New Yorker*, *Vogue* and *Harper's*. As the right people began to come, Grace insisted that every cent of profit be put into the renovation and beautification of the hotel. She threw out all the furniture in the public areas.

"Rattan might be fine for island houses, but our guests want antiques and polished wood," she said. Rick sighed, but ordered from London and Paris. When things arrived, he had to admit that they turned the foyer from a pleasant island bar into a smashing contemporary statement of the Caribbean.

And Grace still hadn't taken a penny in salary. Rick confronted her one day. "Listen," he said. "It's not right. It can't go on like this."

She turned her large eyes up to him. "What can't?"

"You're treating this like a charity," he said. "Every client that's here now is here because of you. You have to get something out of it."

"Oh, but I have," she said with the ghost of a smile.

"Like what?"

"A reason to start living again," she said. "When you lose the person you love, it seems as if life is completely meaningless. I didn't even want to get up in the mornings … but then, a person like you wouldn't understand that."

"You're wrong there," he said. "I understand it very well."

She flushed. "Of course, your parents' death. That was very tactless of me. I always seem to say the wrong thing where you're concerned."

It occurred to him then that no one else knew about Contessa and what he had been going through. He would have liked to confide in someone, especially someone as cool and rational as Grace, but he was scared she'd make some crushing remark about his always falling for the wrong women. She did this pretty often, he noticed. She always seemed to know when he'd been down to the bars, and there had been the incident, a few nights before, at the hotel.

He had been to the Coq d'Or and met a stunning Swedish blonde who had been only too willing to come up and see the famous Trade Winds hotel. She was happily drunk on rum punches and giggling slightly as Rick steadied her across the foyer, when he noticed Grace still at work at one of the tables. Grace's face flushed with annoyance when she saw him.

"Can I speak to you a minute?" she demanded.

"Does it have to be now?" He indicated the swaying Swedish beauty.

"Yes, right now."

"Okay." He put the girl into the nearest armchair. "Don't go away. I'll be right back. My manager needs to speak to me," he said with a frown in Grace's direction.

"Okay, what?" he demanded as he approached her.

"I just wondered if you'd lost all sense of reason," she said quietly.

"Meaning what?"

"Bringing that ... bimbo up here, in full view of everybody."

His face flushed. "Hey, I get time off, you know, and what I do with my own time is my business."

"Not when you own a classy hotel. Bringing a cheap woman like that into the main lobby lowers the tone of the whole place."

Rick started to laugh. "I do believe you're jealous," he said.

"Don't be ridiculous."

"Then why are you so upset?"

"Because I care about the reputation of the hotel," she said. "I'm not having you blow everything because you can't keep your hands off anything with makeup and cleavage."

"You suggest I become a monk?" he asked, his eyes challenging hers. "I'm a man, you know. I have all the normal male urges."

"Then please keep them out of sight of the guests," Grace said, "or they'll think they've wandered into the Pink Pussycat instead of Trade Winds."

This made Rick laugh even more. "Very good, ma'am," he said. "I'm obeying orders, ma'am. No more public displays of lust. No sex in the lobbies. I'll take her down to one of the bungalows, ma'am." And he gave a mock salute as he turned back to the blonde.

"Damn him," Grace said as she watched him go. She was annoyed with herself that she cared how Rick behaved. She didn't want to be attracted to him, but she couldn't help it. He was just so gorgeous and it was about time she had a man in her life again. Andrew had found her desirable and exciting. Why then didn't Rick even seem to notice that she was a woman?

Rick had surprised himself that night by driving the girl home instead of taking her to his bungalow. He wondered why he cared so much what Grace thought. After all, it was only a business partnership, wasn't it? He didn't need her approval for what he did after hours. Seeing him with that girl had really seemed to upset her. Could it be possible that lovely, cool Grace was jealous after all? Rick smiled to himself. One day he was going to find out if there was a warm heart beating under that cool exterior.

In the days that followed, there was little opportunity for private life of any sort. The hotel was miraculously full and he and Grace worked like maniacs. He had discovered the down side of attracting the rich and spoiled: They liked to be pampered twenty-four hours a day. The new guests thought nothing of calling room service for eggs Benedict at two in the morning, or to have a Monopoly set sent up at midnight because they were bored.

Late one night Grace slumped down beside Rick on the wrought iron bench outside the front door. Her normally immaculate hair was plastered to her forehead with sweat and her peach silk dress hung limp against her body.

"I've had it," she said. "My muscles are so sore and tired, I can't move another inch."

"Did you find the right brand of cat food Mrs. Taylor wanted for Fifi?" Rick asked with a grin.

"We're having it flown in tomorrow," Grace said. "For tonight Fifi had to make do with shrimp and lobster tail."

"Poor underprivileged cat, but you've only yourself to blame. Your advertisements brought her here."

Grace sighed. "Even I didn't think the place would do so damn well."

"Don't swear. It lowers the tone of the place," Rick said with a triumphant grin.

"It's your bad influence. I never swore until I met you."

He got up. "What about extending my bad influence and having a drink?" he said. "I could mix us both one of my Paradise Rum specials."

"That sounds great," she said, "although I don't know if I should drive home after drinking one. They're lethal."

"Then stay the night," he said.

He hadn't meant his remark to have sexual overtones and he realized only after he had said it that she might take it the wrong way. But she was so tired, she didn't even notice.

"I might do that," she said. "I've been thinking that I spend so much time with you, it's like being married."

Rick paused in the doorway and stood, looking down at her. "You know, that's not such a bad idea," he said.

"What isn't?"

"Getting married. You and I."

"But we don't love each other."

"We could learn to, I think," he said. He went over to her and perched on the arm of her chair. "But that doesn't even matter. We're good for each other, you and I. We're on equal footing. We certainly achieve great things together. You've made this place what it is …."

"And so the reward is to marry poor, lonely me?" There was hurt in her eyes.

"I put it badly," he said. "I think I want to marry you, Grace. I've gotten used to having you around. I know what you're thinking. I know it's not one of those incredible passions, but those things burn themselves out. I really think we have something we could build on, that would last. Think of it as good for the hotel."

"So it's essentially a business proposition?" she said cautiously.

"You made me a business proposition that turned out to be just right," he said. "Now it's my turn. What do you say?"

"And what about your little trips to the Coq d'Or?" she asked quietly. "I don't share, you know."

"I wouldn't need them anymore if I had someone who mattered to me," he said simply. "No more blondes in bikinis, I promise you."

"Huh," she said. " I wish I could believe you."

"So you were jealous?"

"Of course. I was damned jealous. How do you think it made me feel, watching you walk past me every night with a different woman, as if you never knew I existed?"

He pulled her to her feet, taking her into his arms. "Grace, you really do like me!" he said.

"Of course I do, you idiot. You're a very desirable man, as you well know, and I'm only human too."

She raised her lips to his and he kissed her, hesitantly at first, then with passion that surprised him.

"We'll make a great couple, Grace. We'll fly to the mainland and get married right away!"

"There's just one thing," she said, breaking away from his embrace.

"Which is?"

"I want a legal contract giving me fifty percent of the hotel."

"You what?"

"It's very simple, Rick. I've been left with nothing once before. It's not funny and it's never going to happen again. I have to protect myself this time. I want to be the legal owner of a fifty-percent share in Trade Winds."

Rick gazed into her eyes. They were very lovely eyes, sensitive and deep. "All right, Mrs. Sommers," he said, "forty-five percent for you, fifty-five for me. I want the last word."

"You got yourself a deal," she said.

CHAPTER 13

The small plane rose above the clouds to level off in the blue sky above. The seat belt sign was turned off and Grace reclined her seat with a sigh of content.

"Happy?" Rick murmured in Grace's ear as the plane reached its cruising altitude en route back to St. Martin.

Grace nodded.

"It was a good honeymoon, right?"

Grace nodded again, sleepily, and rested her head on his shoulder. Good was an understatement. It had been an incredible honeymoon, a quite unexpectedly wonderful discovery for both of them. Right up to the moment they entered the judge's chambers in Marigot, she had been having second thoughts about marrying Rick. The rational part of her whispered that she was crazy: This man was a womanizer who had never shown any previous attraction to her. He was marrying her because she was a good asset for the hotel. The romantic side of her argued that she wanted Rick Sommers and really felt something for him. She was sure she could turn him into the kind of man she wanted. If she kept him interested enough in bed, he'd never have to look anywhere else. He would be the kind of loyal, trustworthy man she longed to grow old with.

Grace closed her eyes and gave a small, contented sigh. Neither of them could have predicted the way the honeymoon would turn out. Rick had kissed her gently on the cheek after the marriage ceremony, but that had been their only contact. They had sat, side by side, nervously making small talk on the plane to St. Lucia and then, when they were shown into the rustic cottage by a waterfall at the mountain resort, she had seen the tension on Rick's face. She decided that perhaps they had made a big mistake. He wasn't attracted to her at all. He didn't even want to touch her. Any interest she had felt from him these past few weeks must have been in her imagination.

She took off her corsage.

"So, do you want to go down to dinner first?" he asked her.

"Sure. Whatever you want."

He looked around. "I'd like to go for a walk through the woods, I think."

"Okay, let's go." She kicked off her high heeled sandals and put on flats.

She saw Rick smile, as if he appreciated her willingness to please. For a while they walked along the trail. It was cool beneath the tall trees. Ferns hung down from ancient trees and the river danced beside them, splashing over moss covered boulders.

"It's beautiful here," Grace said. "So unlike the tropics. It reminds me of Switzerland."

"I know, it's hard to think we are still in the Caribbean," he said. "Do you miss things like Switzerland, England, France?"

"Not when I'm busy," she said. "And happy where I am."

They came to a little wooden bridge across a creek. Rick paused on it, looking down into the water. "Look, Grace," he said hesitantly, "maybe we're both expecting too much from this. We're both still getting over a loss in our lives. You're trying to get by without Andrew. I'm still grieving for my parents, but there's more that you should know. There was a woman too. It's all over and she's gone. I'm trying to forget her, but it's going to take a while. So I'm asking you to be patient. I'm going to try hard to be a good husband to you and to make you happy, but give me time, okay? "

She stared down at the water too, watching its steady flow wash over the banks. A brilliant flash of blue appeared as a kingfisher skimmed the surface. She almost laughed. They were in one of the most romantic places on earth and here was a man telling her he wasn't in the mood. "Are you saying it was a mistake to come here?" she asked.

"No. I'm just saying … I can't predict how things will turn out."

She looked at him and laughed. "Oh, I see. This all comes down to your ego. You're just warning me in advance that you may not live up to your reputation this evening!"

He looked embarrassed, but he laughed too. "Something like that," he said.

"Don't worry about it," she said. "If we just enjoy the scenery and have some great meals, I'll be happy here. We've got plenty of time."

He took her hand. "Thanks, Grace," he said.

They walked back hand in hand to the cabin. After dinner she let Rick shower first. When she came out of the shower with a towel wrapped around her, he was lying back on the bed, just wearing pajama bottoms, staring up at the ceiling.

"Shower felt good, right?" he said.

"Great." She came over to him and released the towel. Then she climbed onto the bed.

"Did I ever mention," she said huskily, "that showers cool most people down, but they warm me up."

She closed her eyes and just let it happen ....

"My goodness, Grace," he murmured when it was over. "Where did you learn to do that?"

She gave him a long, satisfied smile as she slid off him and lay beside his muscled body. "Next time it's your turn," she said.

And after that it seemed that the whole honeymoon had turned into a next time. They made love and slept briefly, occasionally appearing for meals. Now they couldn't be close to each other without touching and couldn't touch each other without becoming aroused. Grace opened her eyes and smiled as she felt Rick's hand on her knee. Remembering the past week made her ache for him once again.

"You have to wait until we get home," she said.

"Pity." He glanced around at the rest of the cabin.

"Don't even think about it."

"I can't help thinking about it," he said. "You're an incredible woman, Grace. I can't believe how lucky I was to marry you."

"You're not so bad yourself, Rick Sommers, " she said.

"We're going to make Trade Winds into a truly great hotel."

"The best. The only Michelin Five Star property in the Caribbean," she said.

"If we ever manage to get out of bed," he whispered.

When they arrived home, Grace unpacked while Rick went through the mail. "More congratulations from the Van Baarens and Duykers," he said. "It's incredible how quickly news spreads on an island this size. We thought we could slip away and be married in secret and it seems that everyone knows … oh …"

Grace looked up, detecting something in the tone of his voice.

"What is it?"

He put on a bright tone. "It's an invitation from Christof."

"Christof Philips?"

"Yes. He wants to give a party for us up at Plantation House."

"How nice of him. You must know him well."

"Very well. He's been like a second father to me."

"You don't look very excited about it."

Rick shrugged. "Oh, no, it will be fine. It's just that big parties aren't my idea of fun," he said as he moved over to embrace her. His lips brushed along her neck as she laughed.

"We have to go if he's giving it in our honor," she said, pushing him away."

"Of course," Rick said. "We'll go."

"When is it?" Grace took the letter from him. "Oh, it's next Saturday. I wonder if I have time to buy a new dress? I don't suppose I can fly to San Juan. I wonder what the selection is like on the island. I want to make a good first impression. I understand they are pretty rich."

"Very rich."

"Then I have to have a new dress."

"You look great no matter what you wear," he said.

She laughed. "Typical husband remark."

"In your case it's true. You have a way with clothes. You can take something simple and make it look really classy …."

"Unlike Christof's daughter-in-law," Grace laughed.

"Who?"

"The one who calls herself Contessa," Grace said. "Contessa, my foot. I don't think she ever saw the inside of an Italian palazzo! I saw her in the market the other day— completely overdressed, cleavage down to her ankles, and jewelry everywhere." Rick didn't say anything as she went on. "I hear that she's actually an exgangster's girl who latched on to Robert in New York."

"Who told you that?" Rick demanded.

She looked up, surprised at the sharpness of his voice. "It's the gossip that's going around. I don't know where I heard it. Maybe it was one of the maids."

"You shouldn't listen to gossip. Especially on an island like this!" Rick said.

She sensed his anger and came over to rest a hand on his shoulder. "Do you know her, then?"

"Yes," he said. "As a matter of fact, she rented one of my bungalows when she first came to the island."

"So it's not true—all the stuff about the Mafia?"

"Her first husband was connected with the Mafia," he said, "but she didn't know that when she married him. She's had a very hard life and she's a sweet person underneath it all."

She laughed uneasily. "Okay, I'll reserve judgment until I meet her," she said, "although I have to tell you right now that she doesn't look like my type."

"Nobody's asking you to be best friends with her," Rick said. "Just be nice. Christof Philips has always been very kind to me and Robert is my friend. We're going to be socializing at the same affairs whether you like her or not."

She gave him a sweet smile. "Don't worry, I'll be my normal, charming self when we meet," she said.

He laughed now. "I've seen how charming you can be when you want to on our first meeting," he said. "That's what scares me."

"How do I look?" Contessa turned to Robert inquiringly.

"Stunning, my darling."

"You always say that and I don't look stunning at all. I look fat!" She ran her hands over her swollen belly.

Robert smiled adorningly. "You still look stunning to me. Motherhood agrees with you. You look gorgeous."

Contessa made a face. "I don't think I want to go to Christof's party," she said. "Can I plead morning sickness?"

Robert looked surprised. "Not go? Of course you have to go. Rick's bringing his new wife over and we have to make them welcome." He put a hand on her shoulder. "It's especially important that you two should become friends.

Paradise Rum is going to be taking more and more of my
time. You need a woman friend, especially at a time like
this ...."

Contessa winced. She was thinking that it would hardly
be tactful to become best friends with the wife of her former lover and father of her child. Besides, being friends
with Grace would mean being around Rick, and she didn't
know whether she could handle that. On the other hand,
she knew that what Robert said was true. He was very
busy with Paradise Rum and she was incredibly lonely. She
and Marigot hadn't hit it off that well. She had tried, but
Robert had made it very clear that he didn't want to socialize with Will and his native wife. Besides, Marigot had her
mother and sister right there. It would be very comforting
to have a woman friend to talk to.

She imagined them shopping together when she'd finally got her figure back, trading makeup and recipes and
indulging in the sort of girl-talk that had been denied to
her since she married Joseph. Joseph had never let her get
close to anybody. When any of her girlfriends from her
childhood had come to call, Joseph had sent them away. He
hadn't even let her spend too much time with her mother,
and she missed the closeness. If Grace turned out to be a
good friend, she would force herself to put any memories
of Rick behind her and get on with her role as a wife and
mother.

She looked at herself critically in the mirror: Was the
tangerine fabric too bright? It certainly accentuated her
hair, but it also accentuated her breasts, which were now
even more magnificent thanks to five months of pregnancy.

Better to play up her best features, she decided, so that nobody looked at the bulge underneath.

She fastened the emerald pendant that Robert had given her as a wedding gift around her neck. There. Now she really looked elegant. Nobody else on the island had an emerald that size! She was still delighting in her new wealth and Robert so enjoyed her childlike pleasure in receiving jewels and trinkets. He couldn't resist constantly surprising her with more.

He came up behind her, looking at her in the mirror as he slid his hands around to cup her breasts. "You're more beautiful than ever," he whispered, kissing her bare shoulder.

Sounds came from down below. Robert peered out of the window. "Oh, that's Rick's car. They've arrived. We better go down."

"You go on down," she said. "I have to finish my make-up."

After he had gone she sat on the bed, trying to compose herself. Could she really pull off facing Rick again so that nobody suspected anything? She had put off revealing her pregnancy until the right moment so that Robert would never ask if the child was his. And she would have to face Rick sometime. For a second the confident face in the mirror faltered. She looked liked the wistful girl staring in Tiffany's window again. If only she'd had a little more time. If only she'd found out about the baby sooner, would she now have been Mrs. Rick Sommers? Would she have been just as happy as she was with Robert? Contessa tossed back her luxuriant hair. No sense in brooding on what might have been. She had made her choice and now she had to live with it, for better or worse.

She put her hair up in a comb to accentuate her long, slender neck and beautiful emerald. She waited until she heard voices move into the hall from outside before she opened her bedroom door.

She saw them all look up at her and noted with pleasure that Rick's eyes widened at the sight of her. Then, very slowly, she descended the staircase.

"Ah, there you are, my dear," Christof said, going to take her hand. "Feeling better now, I hope. Robert said you were a little under the weather."

"Just a little tired, thank you, Christof," she said. "I find the heat so draining in my condition."

"It's draining in anyone's condition at the moment," Robert said. "It's been over ninety all week. I'm almost praying for a tropical storm to form."

"I've had enough hurricanes to last a lifetime, thanks," Rick said. "It's pleasantly cool on the beach where we are."

"Well, you do have the best site on the island," Robert said, his voice laden with hidden meaning as he glanced at his father.

"Introductions are in order," Christof said, clapping his hands. "Will! Marigot! Get out here!"

Will appeared, his arm around a very heavy Marigot.

"Heavens, I hope it's not catching," Rick said with a wink at Grace. Grace blushed, which was unlike her.

Christof stepped up and took her hand. "My family, I want you to meet the wife of someone who is as close to me as my own sons." Robert glanced at Will. "Grace my dear, this is my son, Will and his wife, Marigot. You've already met my son, Robert, and this is his wife, Contessa."

The two women shook hands.

"I'm so happy to meet you, Grace," Contessa said breathlessly. "I've been longing for some company. Marigot is too tired for anything, and I hate spending the days by myself. I'd just love to browse in the market or go shopping with you. Have you been to the market in Marigot yet? You must let me take you soon."

"Thanks, Contessa, but I'm afraid the hotel takes up one hundred percent of my time, as Rick will tell you," Grace said.

Contessa flushed. "Oh," she said. "Rick always seemed to have a little time for fun when I was there."

"Well, we've upgraded the place now," Rick said quickly. "Perhaps you haven't heard what Grace has managed to do. We've completely redecorated and we've got a first class chef. We're fully booked this season. But it means we're on call twenty-four hours a day."

Grace put a hand on his arm. "We're trying to find a manager so we can have a little time to ourselves, but it's not easy. While we were away the man we left in charge upset several important guests and they left early. We can't risk that happening again." She looked up at Rick with the hint of a smile. "Of course, we're not likely to be going on a honeymoon again in the near future ...."

"I'm glad you're doing so well, Rick," Robert said. "We were worried for a while that you wouldn't be able to make a go of the place. It would have been a shame if you'd had to sell."

"It was all Grace's doing," Rick said. "She just has a flair for the right thing. Of course, rubbing elbows with the rich and famous helped." Rick smiled at Grace.

"Oh, did you work for someone of importance?" Contessa asked sweetly.

"What Rick meant was that I moved in the same social circles as the rich and famous," Grace said equally sweetly. "I haven't actually had to work for a living for some time now. That's why I enjoy doing it. It's quite a novelty."

"Let's hope you don't get bored when the novelty wears off, then," Contessa said.

"Oh, I don't think I could ever get bored with Rick around," Grace said.

A brief frown crossed Contessa's face. "Yes, he is an interesting person, isn't he?" she said. "I know he impressed me with all the fascinating things he could do."

Sensing a tension he couldn't explain, Christof spoke up. "Perhaps we should go through and meet the rest of our guests," he said. "We have both Dutch and French officials present tonight. Always a good idea to keep on the right side of both parties, I think." He took Grace's arm and steered her into the living room, open on a night like this to the gardens and breezes behind the house. Robert seated Contessa in an armchair and got her a drink. Christof still had a firm hold on Grace's arm and introduced her to various people. She tried to keep who belonged with whom straight, but there were so many Van Pelts and Van Klomps that she soon became confused and just shook hands with a perpetual smile on her face.

"We're delighted your hotel is doing so well, Mrs. Sommers," Mr. Van Ruyker said as he shook her hand.

"The sort of guests you're attracting now spend more in my duty free shop in town. I had a couple in the other day who bought a whole lot of Waterford crystal and Royal Doulton and had it shipped up to your hotel."

"I hope you're going to start giving us a commission, then, if we send you the customers," Grace said, laughing.

He patted her hand. "Smart girl. No wonder you're doing so well. Let's just say you send me customers and I'll give you a really good rate on anything you need imported."

"It's a deal, Mr. Van Ruyker," Grace said. She had wanted to purchase some good china and crystal for the dining room at the hotel, so this could be very useful. She looked for Rick to tell him about it and saw that Contessa was sitting like a queen in the biggest armchair with Rick standing on one side of her and Robert on the other. As Rick said something she lifted her face to him and Grace saw her eyelashes flutter as she smiled.

"Dinner," Christof said, noticing Madame de Gaulle hovering in the doorway. He took Grace's arm and escorted her through to the dining room, pulling out a chair for her in the center of the table beside his place. Robert took one end of the table and Will the other. Grace noticed that Contessa had taken up position beside Rick. She wondered if that had been Christof's seating arrangement or Contessa had made her own.

The first course was a hot soup.

"This is delicious," Grace said. "What is it?"

"Turtle, of course, speared with my own gun," Christof said proudly.

"Heavens," Grace exclaimed. "I thought turtle soup was

something one only read about in books."

"I should have thought that things like caviar and turtle soup were part of the daily diet in your social circle," Contessa exclaimed.

"There aren't too many turtles swimming around Paris," Grace answered, "and I've spent most of my time in Europe recently. Which reminds me, I've been fascinated by your name. Which part of Italy does your family come from, and where is your ancestral palazzo? Maybe I met them when I was staying with our friend Count Fabrini."

"Excuse me?" Contessa said. "I'm not from Italy. My family comes from New York, although my grandparents came from Sicily, I think."

"Oh," Grace said. "Then you're not really a *contessa*?"

Contessa flushed. "Oh, no. That was just Robert's pet name for me. He called me his Italian Contessa."

"How sweet," Grace said, "and now everyone calls you that. I wish I had a nickname more interesting than Grace. Grace is such an uninteresting name, don't you think?"

"You mean Rick hasn't come up with something endearing for you yet?" Contessa asked. She moved closer to Rick until her shoulder was touching his and covered his hand with her own. "Why haven't you given poor Grace a pet name? I hope you don't have so many other things on your mind that you're not paying her enough attention!"

Rick actually blushed and Grace got the impression that one of the things Contessa thought he'd have on his mind was her.

"I'm paying her enough attention," he said.

"And making her happy?" Contessa demanded.

"And making her happy, I hope."

"That's good, because a woman likes to be satisfied, as you well know." Rick pulled his hand away awkwardly. "I'd better eat my soup, Contessa," he said, "before it gets cold."

Grace watched them both all through the meal. At one point she noticed that Rick was distracted by something going on under the table. She resisted the urge to drop her napkin and look for herself. If that cheap woman wanted to make a public play for her husband, then let her. It was clear he wasn't the least bit interested. She was probably the type who flirted with everybody just to get attention.

After several courses with accompanying wines, the pace of the meal had slowed considerably. Guests were involved in conversation all around the table. Contessa rose to her feet. "If you'll excuse me, Christof, I have to go and lie down," she said. "I get tired so easily at the moment, and all my energy seems to have drained away. Please excuse me, everybody."

Most people murmured sympathy, but Rick said, "Stay and finish the meal, Contessa. It's still early. And you must be hungry. I notice you've been eating for two!"

It was meant as a good-natured joke, but Contessa turned her smoldering tiger eyes on him. "Pregnancy puts a woman's body through a lot of stress, Rick," she said. "You men are such beasts the way you never stop to consider what you might be putting a woman through. You of all people should know that."

Grace watched her grand exit out of the dining room and up the staircase. What on earth had she meant when she said Rick of all people?

CHAPTER 14

"I thought that went pretty well, don't you?" Rick asked as they drove through the gates of Plantation House. Sugarcane rose high on either side of them.

"If you love farce," Grace said coldly.

"Meaning what?"

"You and Contessa."

"That was nothing. She's just naturally friendly."

"Oh, is that what it was? Natural friendliness? I didn't notice. I'd have called it more natural nastiness. It was only you she couldn't keep her hands off."

Rick reached across and put his arm on her shoulders. "Come on , Grace, it was all harmless. Forget it."

Grace swallowed hard. "It would be easy to forget if it was harmless. I got the impression that it wasn't harmless at all. Just what went on between you and Contessa?"

Rick sighed. "Okay. I suppose you should know the truth. We had a very brief affair when she was staying at Trade Winds. It was nothing. All over and forgotten."

"She doesn't seem to have forgotten it," Grace said, "and I don't think you have either."

They drove on in silence, their headlights creating an arc of light through the dark mountain road. Grace found herself holding her breath. She wanted to hear the truth, but at the same time she was afraid. She was scared he was going to admit that he still loved Contessa. The lights of Oyster Pond and Trade Winds twinkled below them as they dropped down to the coast, and soon they were driving between manicured lawns to the hotel parking lot.

They walked up to their room in silence. Rick sat on the bed and started to take off his shoes. Grace couldn't stand the tension any longer. They had to get this out in the open right now or it would fester between them forever. She had to know, however painful the truth was.

She had her back turned to him as she said, "She was the one, wasn't she?"

"What do you mean?"

"You know what I mean, Rick. When we were first married you told me you were still getting over a woman. She was the woman."

"Yes," he said slowly. "She was the one—I thought I was in love with her. But then Robert came back and she chose all that lovely Paradise Rum money."

"I see," Grace said. She stepped carefully out of her dress and hung it up, still turned away from him.

He got up and came over to her. "No, you don't see at all, Grace." He put his hands on her shoulders and turned her around to face him. "The truth is that I didn't expect to love you. I liked you, I admired you, and I thought we'd make a great team, but I never expected to fall in love with you the way I have."

Slowly she raised her eyes to meet his.

"I love you, Grace," he said. "Whatever went on in my

life before doesn't matter now. It's over, forgotten. Now it's just you and me. We're going to have a great life together and we're going to be very, very happy. Someday we're going to have our own family ...."

Grace blushed again.

"What is it? You're against having kids?" he asked. "We never spoke about it, I know ..."

"Oh, no, it's not that," she said. "It's just that I wasn't sure that I wanted them so soon."

"That's okay. We can wait. We're both young."

"I'm not sure we can wait," she said, biting her lip with embarrassment.

"Why not?"

"I've always been very regular," she said. "I know it's too soon to tell yet, but I am a couple of days late ...."

Rick's face lit up. He took her in his arms. "Hey, that's wonderful. That's incredible. We'll show those Philipses they're not the only ones who can make babies, right? Our kid's going to swim better and sail better and throw the football better than theirs."

She laughed at his boyish excitement. "It might be a false alarm, Rick, and it also might be a girl."

"Nah," he said. "We have to have a boy first."

"Rick Sommers, you are such a chauvinist," she said, laughing, "and there's not much you can do about it either way."

He held her away from him and looked into her eyes with great tenderness. "I suppose a girl would be okay if she looked like you," he said.

Grace freed herself from his grasp. She was suddenly all

business again. "If it is true and I am pregnant, then we've got to get busy right now," she said. "I'm not going to have time or energy once the baby arrives, so we've got to finish upgrading the hotel before then."

"I thought it was upgraded," Rick exclaimed.

"As they say in the movies, baby, you ain't seen nothing yet. We're just starting to bring in guests with class, Rick. This is when we should take the time to turn the hotel into a real showplace. We need a proper swimming pool ...."

"We've already got one, and the ocean's only two steps away."

"That rinky-dink little thing isn't good enough. We want a spectacular pool with waterfalls, and we really should replace that roof before next hurricane season, and we should put in a dock for water sports—get some little sailboats and pedalos and scuba gear so that the guests are never bored."

Rick held up his hand. "Hey, slow down. We're talking big bucks here," he said. "It was one thing to start putting fresh flowers on tables and to put new bedspreads on, but a pool—a roof, a dock? We've done well this season, but not that well. We'd have to go into debt to build all those things."

"Not necessarily," Grace said. "Stay there and I'll be right back."

She ran down to the hotel safe and returned with an aged red leather box.

Rick looked at it with interest. "What have you got there, the crown jewels?" he asked.

"That's right," she said. "How did you guess?"

"Come on, what is it really?"

"It's a set of jewelry that once belonged to a Russian empress," she said. She opened the box. A matched set of rubies and diamonds flashed in the lamplight. Rick whistled. "You weren't kidding, were you? My God, where did you get them?"

"Andrew gave them to me as a present on the night he died," Grace said, her face growing sad at the memory of his death. "I should imagine they'd fetch enough at auction to finish all the improvements we want to make on the hotel," Grace said.

"I can't let you sell your jewels," Rick said. "I know I'll never be able to replace them for you."

"It's okay," she said with a wistful smile. "When would I ever get an opportunity to wear a necklace like this on an island? It hardly goes with beach attire, does it?"

"But Grace, they're unique. They're so beautiful. It wouldn't be right to turn them into cold cash and a new roof."

"Rubies won't keep out the rain," Grace said. "Look, Rick, I'm offering them freely. I didn't have to tell you about them, but I have. I want to sell them. I want to make our hotel the most luxurious, elegant resort in the entire Caribbean. It would make me happy to know they'd been put to good use."

She held out the box to him. "Here, take them, "she said. "I don't know how one proceeds with selling something like this. Maybe you'll have to go to London or Paris?"

Very reluctantly Rick took the box from her. "I really don't like doing this," he said.

"Why not?"

Rick frowned. "I'm the man. I should be providing for you."

"Oh, bull. Men have married women for their money since the beginning of time. And if we're going to have a good marriage, we provide for each other. Now, no more damn arguing."

Rick shook his head, but he was smiling. "Don't swear," he said. "It lowers the tone of the place."

The next day, after many phone calls, Rick found that Sotheby's had a permanent representative in New York and he flew up there with the jewels. He had already decided that Grace shouldn't have to give up her whole set. It was clear that the necklace, with its impressive center pendant, was the most valuable item of the set. The teardrop earrings also contained large, valuable rubies. He privately decided to sell only these two and put the bracelet and ring back in the safe. Grace should have some memento of the time she lived a life of glamour and riches!

Simon Smithers, the Sotheby representative, was most impressed.

"Lovely pieces," he said. "I'm sure I can get you a very handsome price at auction. It just depends how rapidly you need the money. If you're prepared to wait awhile, I can take them over to London. One usually finds that the objects command higher prices at our Fall auctions."

"We'd rather like the money quickly," Rick said. "We're in the middle of making improvements to our hotel. The roof has to be finished before next hurricane season."

"Very well, I'll see what I can do," Mr. Smithers said,

"although I can't guarantee instant results. It's not every day a person wants to buy something of this quality."

Rick flew home and reported to Grace.

"I'm not prepared to wait," she said. "You've got me now while I still have energy. Who knows how I'll be in a couple of months—all lazy and lumpy like Contessa!"

"Then you really think you are ... we really are?" Rick asked cautiously.

She nodded. "It seems that way. I've made a doctor's appointment for next week and then I'll know for sure. But I would make odds on it."

Rick beamed again. "My amazing Grace," he said.

She chuckled. "If that's the best you can do for my little pet name, then forget it," she said, mocking Contessa.

Rick slid his arms around her. "You know, Grace, you're not the sort of person a guy can call Pookie or Fluffy."

"Certainly not Fluffy," she said, laughing. "We should see the bank manager in the morning, Rick, and ask about a short-term loan. I'm dying to get started on that swimming pool."

Robert Philips stopped off in New York on his way back from London. Everything about his trip had gone incredibly well. The deal in his pocket would make Paradise the most widely distributed rum in England and Europe. North American sales were climbing steadily. Now all he had to do was tackle the Japanese and persuade them that rum tasted better than sake! The way he felt right now, he was ready for anything. It had been an incredible year. He had graduated with a business degree from Yale, he had married the most beautiful woman in the world, and was due to become a father any day. He looked forward to a new generation of Philipses to carry on and expand the empire. Maybe by the time he handed over the company to his son, they'd own the entire island—hotels and casinos as well as rum.

He felt powerful as he strode down Fifth Avenue. It had been a wise decision to stop over and take their major American distributor out to lunch. Always wise to cement ties. And now he felt fresh and ready to fly back to the island and Contessa.

At Tiffany's window he paused, and old memories came rushing back. He remembered how he had first seen Contessa, staring wistfully at jewels she knew she could never have, and suddenly he made up his mind. He'd buy her an incredible piece of jewelry as a present when she had the baby! He examined the pieces in the window and wished that he had a greater knowledge of gems. They all looked pretty to him, but he had no idea which would increase in value. Always the businessman, this was important to Robert.

A tall, distinguished-looking man standing beside him looked at the window with a faint smile.

"Very pretty, of course," he said, "but a lot of junk."

He had an educated British accent.

"I beg your pardon?" Robert said.

The man smiled. "I was just commenting that this sort of stuff is designed for the American market. Not much lasting value here—too bitty."

"You know about jewelry, then?" Robert asked. He was immediately on the defensive, having his country and his taste put down like this.

"Yes, I do," the man said. "Actually, it's what I do for a living. I acquire pieces for Sotheby's and take them over to auction in London."

"I see. "In spite of himself, Robert was impressed. "And you wouldn't recommend anything in this window?"

The man shrugged politely. "They might have better pieces inside, no doubt, but if you're buying for quality, go for the stone, not the fancy setting. A good stone doesn't need all this frou-frou around it. It speaks for itself. Now, take the ruby necklace I've just acquired: a perfect, flawless, huge center stone and just the right amount of smaller stones leading up to it. An absolute masterpiece. Of course, those old Russians knew about quality."

"It's Russian?"

"Belonged to Empress Marie Fedorovna." He looked shrewdly at Robert. "Are you interested in purchasing jewelry, Mr. … er?"

"Philips," Robert said. "Robert Philips of Paradise Rum. The Brits are very fond of our stuff. I've just returned from London." The man extended his hand. "Simon Smithers. This is indeed a fortuitous meeting, Mr. Philips. If you are serious about buying for investment, then I think you might be interested in this necklace. It comes with matching earrings, which makes it all the more charming. If you care to come to my office …"

Robert needed no urging. After a brief taxi ride he had the necklace in his hands. He imagined the huge teardrop ruby resting on Contessa's smooth white throat.

"I imagine this is not going to come cheaply," he said.

"Of course not," Smithers agreed, "but I could let you have it here at a considerable discount over what I know it would fetch at auction in London. You'd save us the security and advertising costs, you see. We'd be doing each other a favor."

Robert let the gems slip through his fingers, watching as they caught the light. He knew that he had to have the necklace, whatever it cost.

CHAPTER 15

Nine months later, when Ellen Nobel Sommers made her whirlwind entrance into the world, Trade Winds had become the showplace her parents dreamed of. Grace had surprised Rick once more by insisting they raise their prices yet again, to make it even more exclusive. This time Rick hadn't questioned her. Everything she suggested so far had been exactly right. He looked at the hotel with pride as they drove between the great lawns and banks of flowers to the newly stuccoed building. He glimpsed the beautiful sailboats berthed alongside the new docks. He really was the owner of the best hotel on the island!

Rick turned to look at Grace as she sat beside him with baby Ellen in her arms. "Welcome home," he said. "It's a pretty nice home to come back to, isn't it?"

Grace smiled. "It's perfect," she said. "Everything we dreamed of."

"And I've got everything I dreamed of," he said, giving her a fond smile. "Perfect wife, adorable little daughter."

Grace thought she caught a note of false sincerity as he said this. She remembered how much he'd wanted a son. She suspected that it hurt him even more to have produced a daughter after both Marigot and Contessa had given birth to sons. She was still tired and drained from the birth and she felt as if she might cry at any moment. She felt as if this daughter were somehow her fault and she had let him down. Logically she knew that it was his chromosome to blame, but she still felt inadequate. Grace Sommers, architect of a completely renovated hotel and showplace, couldn't produce a son. She looked down at the baby girl in her arms and smoothed back the soft fuzz on the child's head. She really was a lovely baby and perfect in every way. Surely Rick would love her?

The smartly dressed doorman, resplendent in crisp white and gold braid, came running out as the car drew up and saluted as he opened Grace's door. Rick came around to help her out.

"Say hello to the future owner, Samuel," Rick said to the doorman.

"She's going to have you wrapped around her little finger in no time, Mr. Rick," Samuel said, grinning at Rick.

Rick looked down at the baby. "That's entirely possible," he said. "Her mother certainly has."

He put his arm protectively around Grace and the baby as he steered them into the hotel.

Up at Plantation House, Contessa sat on the lawn, beneath the shade of a large tree, and smiled contentedly as she fanned herself. Beside her in a basket lay sturdy young Anthony Phillips, gurgling with delight as he tried to grab his toes. He really was the most handsome baby, she decided; his milk-white skin was in contrast to Will and Marigot's child, named Christofer for his grandfather, who might have passed for an island native. She wondered what Christof thought about his oldest grandson: hardly the image he would have chosen to carry on Paradise Rum! But then, he seemed pleased enough with both grandsons and Robert was absolutely thrilled. He would spend hours staring down at Anthony, examining his little fingers and toes, finding every little thing he did clever and unique. He had never once queried the fact that his child had been born prematurely, after only eight months of marriage. Contessa was very glad that the child had been born with red hair, like most of her family and Robert. If he had been blond and blue-eyed, even Robert might have had his suspicions. Even so, there was something about the way the baby smiled at her that reminded her sharply of Rick. She just prayed that nobody else noticed it.

Little Joey came running up, holding a slightly battered flower.

"I picked it for the baby," he exclaimed.

"Why, thank you, Joey," Contessa said.

Joey nodded solemnly. "Everybody else is giving the baby presents, so I'm giving him a present too."

Contessa felt a stab of guilt. This was the nearest Joey had come to saying that he felt left out after Anthony's birth. She was sure he must be feeling lonely. Everyone who visited Plantation House came with gifts and made a fuss over the baby. No one noticed Joey even existed. And Robert too, who had promised to love Joey as his own, hardly had a glance for the little boy now that Anthony had arrived. She must try harder to make sure Joey felt wanted, or there would be trouble later.

"Here, sweetheart, come and sit by Mommy and I'll read you a story," she said.

"It's okay. I'm going back to Auntie Marigot. She's letting me play in the baby pool with Chris," he said, and ran off again.

Contessa looked across the lawn, and saw Robert and Christof coming up from the factory together, deep in conversation. Two faces lit up when they noticed her.

"Here she is, looking more lovely than ever," Robert said, going over to give her a kiss.

"And here's my handsome grandson," Christof said.

"He's been trying to catch his toes all morning," Contessa said.

Robert squatted down beside him. "Isn't it early for that sort of coordination? Was Chris trying to catch his toes at four months?"

Christof laughed and slapped him on the back. "That's right, Robert. Your child is the world's biggest genius. Give him a pen and paper—maybe he wants to start working for us."

Robert flushed. "Make fun if you want, Father, but this child is as sharp as a tack."

"Both my grandsons take after me in the brains department," Christof said. "In a couple of weeks time I'm going to start teaching them about rum production."

"Which reminds me, Father," Robert said. "Tell Contessa what you've got planned."

"A party of course," Christof said. "I decided to throw a big party for the babies. Now that Rick and Grace are home with their little one, I thought we should have an official coming-out party for the babies to meet each other and the island to meet the babies."

Contessa must have winced, because Robert said, "You don't like the idea? I thought you loved parties."

"Yes, but I'm still kind of tired," she said, "and Grace Sommers doesn't like me."

"That's ridiculous," Robert said. "Who could not like you?"

"She doesn't," Contessa said. "She thinks I'm dumb because I can't run a hotel the way she does. "

"Of course she doesn't, sweetheart," Robert said. "And you are the most perfect wife and mother. I wouldn't want you any other way."

She raised her hand to him and he brought it to his lips.

"Anyway, this party is for the babies," Christof said, trying to cheer her. "They should get to know each other as soon as possible. They're all going to grow up together, just the way Robert, Will, and Rick did."

"Good idea, Father," Robert said. He bent down to Contessa. "And whose baby do you think will be the most adorable?" he whispered. Suddenly he had an idea. This would be the perfect moment. "Wait here. There's a present I've been saving for you. Don't go away."

He sprinted up to the house. Christof shook his head. "I haven't seen Robert run like that in years. It will do him good to have a little son to play with."

"Two little sons," Contessa corrected Christof . "Joey's already old enough to play with him. I just hope he won't forget about Joey completely now that Anthony has arrived."

Christof patted her hand. "We're all very fond of Joey," he said. "Don't worry. You have a husband who always does the right thing."

Contessa watched, intrigued, as Robert came back carrying a red leather box. "Here," he said. "I was waiting for just the right time to give this to you, and I guess this is it."

Slowly she opened the box and gasped as the sun flashed from the diamonds and glowed in the rubies. "Robert!" she exclaimed. "You shouldn't have. This is—" She was speechless.

"Nothing's too good for you, my love," he said. "It once belonged to an empress. Now it belongs to the queen of my heart."

"Oh, Robert …" She was still lost for words. She held up the necklace, completely in awe. "I'll be scared to wear it," she said at last. "What about thieves?"

"It's insured," Robert said, "and we'll keep it in the company safe when you're not wearing it. You can wear it for the party."

Suddenly the party didn't seem like such a bad idea after all. Her son would be the prettiest baby there, and she would be wearing a necklace that any woman would envy. She pictured the admiring glances as she came down the stairs.

"That's right," she said. "I can wear it for the party."

The more she thought about it, the better it sounded. Christof was right. It was a good time for reconciliation. Maybe she had been nasty to Grace. Maybe Grace hadn't meant to snub her at all. Everything had changed now. They all had beautiful babies and it would be so much nicer if they could share experiences as the children grew up. Contessa made up her mind to be extra nice to Grace at the party.

"I hope this is going to go well," Grace said as they drove up to Plantation House.

"Of course it will. Why shouldn't it?"

"Contessa and I didn't exactly hit it off the last time Christof gave one of his parties," Grace said.

"This will be different," Rick said. "Now you're all mothers together. You can all ooh and ahh over each other's kids and discuss diapers and bottles."

"I hope so," Grace said, glancing down at the sleeping child in her arms.

"Of course you will," Rick said. "It's a good time to make peace if there was any bad feeling. All these kids have got to grow up together."

Grace smiled. "You're right. And maybe I was too thin-skinned before. I'll be completely charming to Contessa, however much she annoys me."

Rick grinned to himself as he reached the main entrance and came around to help his wife and daughter from the car.

Once inside the main room, everyone crowded around, admiring the baby and offering congratulations. Will and Marigot came up with baby Chris squirming on Will's shoulder.

"Heavens, he's so big," Grace exclaimed.

Marigot smiled. "It's hard to believe they grow so fast," she said. "He's just learned to crawl, so he hates being held."

Chris let out a piercing scream and Marigot whisked him out of the room. Will wiped his forehead. "Talk about active," he said.

"A future athlete, just like his dad," Rick said. Grace noticed the wistful note in his voice as if he would have liked to have bragged about his son at that moment.

"Where's little Anthony?" Grace asked, looking around.

"They're all up in their room, waiting for Contessa to finish getting ready, I should imagine," Will said.

"Waiting to make a grand entrance, more like it," Grace commented, and got a warning frown from Rick.

Almost on cue the upper doors opened and Contessa came out. She paused on the top step as there was an impressed gasp from the crowd beneath. She began to walk slowly down the stairs, followed by Robert with Anthony on his arm. She was wearing a simple black strapless dress that revealed the top half of exquisitely domed breasts and the already tiny waist beneath. Her hair was piled up off her face and at her throat the beautiful necklace sparkled and glittered. She came down the steps slowly, smiling like visiting royalty, savoring the moment.

At first Grace thought this was just another one of Contessa's grand entrances. She told herself to be amused by it: The woman was a ham and she obviously got a lot of pleasure out of playing to an audience. Contessa reached the bottom of the stairs and was swallowed up by the guests. Grace waited patiently over by the French doors for the royal procession to reach her.

At last Contessa emerged from the crowd.

"Grace!" she said, holding out her hands.

"Congratulations on your little daughter. I hope you've brought her with you, I'm dying to see her."

Grace froze. In disbelief she stared at the ruby lying against Contessa's throat. Contessa was wearing her necklace. In a flash she saw it all: Contessa had somehow gotten word that she was selling her jewelry and had acquired it for herself, waiting for a moment like this to display it. This event had been planned as her moment of triumph! She was showing Grace who was queen of the island.

Grace felt that she was about to explode with anger. As Contessa tried to embrace her, she pushed her away. "How dare you," she snapped. "Just keep away from me!" She shook herself free of Contessa and stepped out into the garden. Contessa followed.

"What's the matter with you? What's wrong?" Contessa demanded.

"As if you didn't know! You had this whole event planned, didn't you! The grand entrance wearing those jewels!" Grace was no longer attempting to keep her voice down. People around them stopped talking and turned to watch. "You were just waiting for this, weren't you? Talk about trying to score points."

"I don't know what you're talking about," Contessa yelled. "What points?"

"To show that you're somehow better than me!"

"That wouldn't be hard, honey," Contessa shouted. "I think it's obvious."

"Well, I've got news for you, Contessa," Grace shouted back. "You might think you're queen of the island, but real royalty has class. You might have the cash, Contessa, but you sure don't have class."

Contessa gave a little cry of rage and flung herself at Grace. Rick, who had come in halfway through this and hadn't a clue what was going on, stepped in between the women. "Whoa," he said. "Cool it, ladies. This is a party. Everyone's watching."

Grace became aware of people staring at her. She couldn't believe she had made a scene in public, and she was scarlet with embarrassment. She turned to Rick. "Get the baby and take me home right now," she begged. "I'm not staying in this house a second longer."

"Under the circumstances, I think that would be the wisest thing," he said. "I don't know what happened here, but I'd rather not wait to find out." He grabbed her arm and whisked her through the French doors and out of the room.

Contessa stood staring after them with tears in her eyes. What could she possibly have done to offend Grace this time? She had tried really hard to be nice and Grace had been unpardonably rude to her. It was all Grace's fault. Robert had now reached her side.

"What is it, darling? What happened here?" he asked in a soothing voice.

Contessa turned a tear-stained face to him. "I hate Grace Sommers," she said. "I'm going to get even with her if it's the last thing I do."

CHAPTER 16

After the incident at the party, Grace made sure that she stayed away from Contessa. Her first impression of the woman had been confirmed. She was a low-class selfish women. But Grace also realized that Contessa was potentially dangerous too. The Philips family was powerful on the island. Grace didn't think that Contessa would be above spreading rumors to bad-mouth the hotel or making some other sort of trouble for them. Rick still didn't seem to understand what the fuss was all about. She had willingly put the necklace up for sale and, by chance, Contessa had purchased it. Actually, he had found out later from Christof that Robert had surprised her with it. Christof had been equally bewildered by the incident, urging Rick to make everything right between the families again. But Robert was now cool to him, and it was apparent that neither Grace nor Contessa was in a hurry to forgive or forget.

Grace noted that Rick always leapt to Contessa's defense. Suddenly she became scared that he still carried a torch for her. Although she found the woman flashy and outrageous, she could see what men saw in her. She was undeniably voluptuous and she radiated sex appeal. Grace felt very inadequate when she looked at herself in the mirror. When she first met Rick she had a slim, athletic body and a great tan. Now she looked pale and washed-out, the sort of woman men pity and pamper but do not desire.

"It's not as if it's my fault," she told herself. And it wasn't. Four months after Ellen's birth she became pregnant again. Rick made jokes that he had only to wink in her direction and she got pregnant. He seemed quite excited over this second child. Grace was not excited at all. She was still recovering from Ellen's birth and this second pregnancy left her feeling completely exhausted. She was stricken with morning sickness that lasted most of the day and she felt dizzy when she tried to walk any distance. The doctor told her to take it easy and lie down, but Grace was not used to idleness. What irked her most was that she was unable to share Rick's life with him. With Ellen they had worked together right up until the birth. They had supervised the building of the dock and pool, chosen fabrics for decorations and plantings for the grounds. When they had any spare time they went out sailing or swimming. They had walked together every evening. And now all she could do was see Rick in the isolation of her bedroom. He was gentle and understanding, and spent the evenings at her side, but she could tell that he missed their former life.

As little Anthony approached his first birthday, Contessa was enjoying her freedom again. Her figure was back to its pre-Anthony curves. She felt full of vitality and ready for anything. The nanny Robert had hired for the children was loving and competent, and Contessa was content to leave most of the day-to-day child rearing to her. It was another delight of being rich to have her children brought to her clean and pretty, to play with them for a while and then to hand them back when they got cranky.

She began to spend her days doing what rich people do. Robert bought her a horse and taught her to ride. Rick took her out in his boat and taught her to sail, and she was taking tennis lessons from the handsome pro at the club. It was like a dream: little Laetitia Gambetti, who carried her shopping up two flights, cleaned her own house, made her own clothes, and never went out anywhere fancy had been transformed. She was now Contessa Philips, a woman who could have anything she wanted ... well, almost anything.

As Robert proved his worth, Christof entrusted him with more and more of Paradise Rum. Robert was pleased and proud and began to work with even greater intensity. Before his father retired, Robert wanted to make Paradise Rum the one rum that counted in the entire Caribbean. He was constantly flying between Miami and Puerto Rico and New York, attending trade fairs, making deals, and when he was home, he was working on ideas to modernize the factory and motivate the workers.

All of this meant that he had little time to spend with Contessa, when she had all the time in the world for him. He would give her a quick peck on the cheek before rushing off to work in the morning. Sometimes they lunched together, but his mind was preoccupied with work, and at night he often fell asleep, too tired for lovemaking. He apologized and said things would get better, but they didn't.

More and more Contessa found herself thinking of Rick. However hard she tried, she couldn't forget how incredible sex had been with him. It annoyed her to think that Rick's talents were now wasted on a cold, pale creature like Grace. She had run into Rick that day when she was shopping in Philipsburg.

"How's Grace?" she asked politely.

"Not feeling too well" was Rick's answer. "The doctor told her she has to rest."

"Poor Grace," she said. "But then, she always has been highly strung, hasn't she? She gets upset over nothing."

Rick cleared his throat. "Yes, I'm sorry about the way she behaved at the party. She misunderstood, you see."

"Life must be rather hard for you if she often has these little tantrums," Contessa said.

"Oh, no, Grace isn't like that," he said. "It's just that, at the moment—"

"Oh, heavens, look at the time," Contessa interrupted. "I've got to run. I'm already late for my tennis lesson!" And she knew for once that her exit had the right effect.

And now she couldn't get him out of her mind. Had she imagined that he had looked at her with longing and regret? Was he really happy with a wife who had to rest all the time? She went down to the stables and had Marcel saddle up Shara, the beautiful bay horse Robert had bought for her.

"Do you want me to accompany you, Madame?" Marcel asked, but Contessa shook her head. "I'll be fine, thank you," she said. "I'm just taking Shara out to stretch her legs."

Once away from Plantation House, she had cut through the cane fields, emerging where a trail dropped down to

Oyster Pond. Trade Winds looked so pretty and inviting, lying in its sparkling bay. A slow smile crossed Contessa's face as she urged the horse on.

Rick was having problems with the swimming pool pump. The new pool equipment was much more complicated than the old had been. One little leaf in the filter and everything seemed to go wrong. He wiped the sweat from his eyes and swore as he loosened the last nut with the wrench and eased the top off the filter. A slick film lay over the surface of the water, and Rick had a hunch the guests' suntan oil was responsible for a lot of the problems he'd been having. But he could hardly ask his guests to stop using suntan oil. He'd just have to resign himself to constant maintenance, as if he didn't have enough to do around the place.

A guest dove into the pool, sending a sheet of spray in his direction. As he felt the spray tingle on his body, he realized that this was the closest he had come to enjoying the water in quite awhile. Life had turned into one long grind of hard work, made even harder now that Grace wasn't able to do her share. He closed the cap on the filter, giving it a savage thump, and was heading across to the maintenance shed when he heard his name being called.

At first he didn't see her, and when he looked around, bewildered, he heard her laugh.

"Contessa?"

"Over here, darling," she said.

Then he saw her on the bay horse in the dappled shade of a large tree.

"What are you doing here?" he demanded.

"Nothing. Just exercising my horse. She's getting fat, but

it's no fun riding on my own." She urged the horse out into the sunlight. "What are you doing?"

"Right now?" He wiped the sweat from his face with a grimy hand. "I've just finished fixing the pool filter and now I've got to see whether my fish suppliers managed to find me any lobster. If my guests go without lobster for two days in a row, they suffer from withdrawal symptoms."

Contessa laughed. "Poor Rick. Did you ever realize that success would be so demanding?"

Rick shrugged. "I'd rather be too busy than not busy enough," he said. "It's just that Grace normally handles a lot of this stuff and right now—"

"Poor Grace," Contessa said again. "And poor Rick. No time for fun anymore."

She moved her horse closer to him. "I've got a great idea," she said excitedly. "Come riding with me."

He shook his head. "You must be crazy. I've a million and one things waiting to be done."

"So let them wait half an hour. A brisk ride will do you good and you'll have all the more energy for your work."

"No, Contessa, I can't," Rick said, uncertainly this time. "I really can't take the time."

"I bet those horses of yours don't get enough exercise either," she said. "You want your guests to find your horses in tiptop condition, don't you?"

"Contessa!"

"Please, Rick, come riding with me. It's no fun on my own and Robert's always too busy. Just a quick gallop … we'll ride along the edge of the ocean, right through the surf. Doesn't that sound wonderful?"

Rick nodded. "It does sound pretty good."

"So you'll come?"

"I can't."

"You're being stubborn," she said. "When was the last time you gave yourself a break?"

He thought, then shrugged. "I can't remember."

"See. I'm doing this for your well-being as well as mine, Rick. Just for half an hour, please?"

"Just for half an hour, then."

Contessa beamed. "I thought you'd come. I had your man saddle up the big gray for you."

Rick had to laugh. "You're something else, you know that?"

"Yes, " she said. "I do know that."

The big dappled gelding was standing tacked up and ready to go. Rick swung into the saddle and they clattered out of the stable yard and down the hotel drive. Once outside the hotel grounds they turned onto a narrow sandy track between hibiscus hedges. Contessa looked back at Rick, then urged her horse into a gallop.

"Hey, Contessa. Wait up," Rick called, but her heard her laugh as she disappeared down the winding track ahead. He shook his head as he commanded the gray to follow. The track emerged onto the cliff tops above Oyster Pond. Here the foliage was sparser and there was short, springy turf underfoot. Over the cliff tops Contessa flew, her flame-red hair streaming out in the wind. When they came to a low wall between properties, Contessa didn't slow her horse at all, but jumped it in a giant stride.

"Contessa! Are you crazy?" Rick yelled, and collected

the big gray enough to make a clumsy jump over the wall. There was no real track now, but Contessa's horse plunged on, leaping a brook, skirting boulders. It was all Rick could do to keep up with her. He was not the world's greatest horseman, and he was scared, but strangely excited too. Gradually the land dropped down to the next bay, with salt flats gleaming in the sun. Contessa didn't slacken the pace at all. Her horse forded the stream flowing into the bay and labored across the soft white sand to the water's edge. This was no resort beach. It was a wild tidal stretch, bordered by sea grapes and reeds. Sea gulls took to the air, crying as they approached. Again Contessa looked back at Rick and smiled before spurring her horse into yet another gallop. The tide was out and the horses raced along the hard sand at the water's edge, sending up a curtain of spray behind them. At the far end of the beach another rocky outcrop rose to meet them. Here Contessa suddenly reined in and brought her horse to a halt.

"What's up?" Rick asked.

"I think there's something wrong with his foot."

"I'm not surprised the way you were riding," Rick said. "You are wild today."

"I'm always wild. Or have you forgotten?" she said.

She swung herself easily from the saddle. Rick followed suit and came around to her.

"Which foot?" he asked.

She looked up at him with a bewitching smile. "It doesn't matter which one."

"Meaning what?"

"How else was I going to get you down from your

horse? I didn't want you to go back to the hotel yet."

"Contessa, I'm trying to run a business …."

They were standing in the shade of the cliff, quite alone on the deserted beach. Her eyes held his as she began to walk toward him. "I've never stopped thinking about you, Rick," she murmured, "about the times we had together. We were great together, weren't we?"

She wrapped her arms around his neck. Rick was aroused. The ride had excited him. "Don't tell me that you've forgotten how it was, Rick?"

He swallowed hard. "I haven't forgotten."

She pressed her body against him. "We're all alone here. Nobody to see if we stop for a few minutes to look at my horse's foot."

"Hoof, Contessa," he said, the tension making him laugh nervously.

"On a horse it's called a hoof."

"Hoof, foot, whatever," she said. Her eyes were dark with desire. "Why waste time talking about horses? The sand is so soft and warm, Rick, and we're all alone."

Her lips were moist and parted, ready for him as she raised her mouth to meet his. Their lips crushed together.

They were both breathing hard when he pulled away from her. "I shouldn't be gone too long," he said huskily.

"It's been too long, Rick," she whispered, "too long for both of us. You need someone like me, someone who knows how to give a man what he wants. Poor, weak Grace has to spend all her days resting … what a disappointment she turned out to be, or didn't you really care who took my place?"

Rick was very aroused. Contessa's hands were driving

him insane, but hearing Grace's name shot a great rush of guilt through his haze of desire. It wasn't Grace's fault that she wasn't the exciting, energetic woman he married. She had become pregnant again too soon and her health was in jeopardy. He was responsible. He looked at Contessa's face as she mocked Grace, her eyes triumphant that she finally had him in her power. He took her hands and gently pushed her away from him.

"I'm sorry, Contessa, but this isn't right," he said. "It isn't that I don't want you … God, how I want you … but I can't do this to my wife, and you can't do it to Robert."

"But it would be our little secret, Rick," she whispered. "Who would ever know?"

"I'd know," he said, "and so would you."

He buttoned his pants and walked over to his horse. "I have to be getting back to the hotel," he said. "I'm sure Grace needs me for something."

CHAPTER 17

G race looked up as Rick came into the bedroom. His shirt was dark with sweat and his face and beard were spattered with sand.

"God, you're a mess," she said. "Where were you? I asked Dumas and nobody seemed to know where you had gone."

Rick started to undress, throwing his clothes roughly in the direction of the hamper in the corner. "I decided to take one of the new horses out," he said. "The guests were complaining that he was too strong."

"I see," she said. "You went out all alone?"

"Yeah."

"Honey, you know I don't like you riding alone. What if you were thrown? You could lie there for days and no one would find you."

"Stop worrying about me, I'm fine," he said, "just let me shower and get cleaned up."

"You're all sandy," she said. "Oh, God. You were thrown. I knew it."

"Oh, Grace, please. A lot of sand gets kicked up when you ride," he said. "Don't you believe me?"

"I guess I do. You wouldn't lie to me, would you?" she

asked. He glanced up and caught those cool eyes watching him steadily.

"You're being silly," he said. "God, Grace, it's the first time I've had any sort of exercise in weeks. You don't want me to lose all my muscle tone, do you?" She didn't answer, so he went on. "I've given up sailing. I've given up water-skiing and spearfishing and all the things I used to love. Is it such a crime to go horseback riding once?"

"I suppose not," she said. She knew she couldn't say anything else without sounding petty. She sensed he was hiding something, but she couldn't imagine what. She couldn't force anything out of him, but she was sure he hadn't been riding alone. She had climbed out of bed and gone to the window when she heard the clatter of hooves going down the drive. She could have sworn there were two horses moving into the shade of the trees. She also thought that one of the riders had red hair.

The incident wasn't mentioned again and Rick didn't go out riding again, so Grace tried to put it from her mind. She wondered if she was being petty and jealous to begrudge Rick one brief ride, even if it was with Contessa. After all, they couldn't do much on horseback, could they? Grace told herself that being cooped up with nothing to do was making her crazy. It was only natural that Rick was frustrated and bored right now. He was used to being active and now he was tied down with all the petty details of the hotel. If she started acting like a suspicious, jealous wife, she'd only drive him away. She reasoned that she had little to fear from Contessa. If she wanted to flirt with Rick, what harm could it do? Contessa might be flashy and overdone, but she wasn't stupid. She liked being queen of the island, living up there at Plantation House. She wouldn't do anything to put her relationship with Robert in jeopardy.

For the next few weeks the hotel was full and Rick worked nonstop, falling into an exhausted sleep whenever the guests didn't need him. Grace decided that she had to make an effort to take some of the work off his shoulders. Perhaps she was now well enough to handle all the book-keeping and reservations again—at least she should give it a try. In fact, now that she was into her fifth month, she was beginning to feel better. She still felt wrung out, but she was no longer plagued with constant bouts of dizziness and nausea.

She managed to find a business suit that still fit her and came downstairs to the front office.

"Where's Mr. Rick?" she asked Samuel, who was standing in the front hall.

"Oh, I think he had to go over to Paradise Rum again," Samuel said.

"Again?"

"Yes, Madame. He went to see about a late shipment. They've been late on delivery a few times now."

"I see," she said as her thoughts raced. Just how many times had he gone over to Paradise Rum? And why weren't the shipments ready? Had Contessa found a way to hold up the order so she and Rick had an ongoing excuse …

"Childish!" Grace said to herself. "You're being stupid and childish." And yet she remembered what Aimee had once said, that Rick had trouble sticking to one woman. And he had told her on their honeymoon that it would take him a while to get over Contessa. Despite the heat and her condition, Grace felt cold and clammy all over. She sat down immediately and fanned herself with a magazine. The trouble was she thought she could never come right out and ask him. She had to keep her suspicions to herself, and it was driving her crazy.

Rick Sommers parked the truck in the shade of a tall pine tree and went into the warehouse. A foreman looked up immediately and came over to him.

"Hello, Mr. Sommers. What can I do for you?"

"I've come about that shipment, Lafitte," Rick said. "You were supposed to deliver five cases the other day and they never arrived."

"Oh, yes, the boys told me. I'm sorry about that. They were stacked with a shipment for a cruise ship by mistake," he said.

"I thought I'd better come by and pick them up myself," Rick said. "I'm down to my last few bottles and I think there would be a mutiny among my guests if we ran out of rum punches."

Lafitte grinned. "There certainly would, Mr. Rick," he said. "I'll have them loaded onto your truck right away."

"Thanks, Lafitte," Rick said.

He walked back to the truck, intending to drive it around to the warehouse door. As he put his hand on the door handle, slim white fingers graced with a large diamond ring stopped him.

"Hi, Rick," Contessa said.

She was wearing skimpy yellow shorts and a matching halter top.

"Hi, Contessa," he said.

"I'm glad you came to see me. I was hoping you'd change your mind."

"I didn't come up to see you," he said. "I drove up here to pick up some rum your husband's company forgot to ship me."

She smiled sweetly. "You could have sent up any old body to pick up a few bottles of rum," she said. "You must have had a small desire to see me, or you wouldn't have come."

"My staff were all busy."

"Oh, sure."

Her eyes were mocking him now, but flirting with him at the same time.

"It's useless to fight it, you know," she said. "We're irresistibly drawn to each other." She put one foot up on the running board of his truck, trapping him against his door. "So, when are we going to go riding again?"

Rick looked around nervously. If Robert were to come out of the office now ...

Contessa read his thoughts. "Oh, it's okay. He's in Philipsburg for the day, meeting with the new cruise line reps. Did you know that soon every cruise ship in the Caribbean will be stocking Paradise rum?" She ran her tongue over her lips. "And you didn't answer my question. When are you and I going to go riding again?"

"Uh ... Contessa, I don't think—" he began, but she interrupted him.

"You could use the exercise, Rick." She tweaked playfully at his waist.

"Ow," he said. "Don't worry about me. I'm as fit as I always was."

"When I said more exercise, I meant the right sort of exercise," she said seductively. "I bet you're not getting enough of that to satisfy your needs."

Rick turned to her and put his hands on her shoulders. "Look, Contessa, I want you to get one thing straight. I am not going riding with you again. It was foolish of us to go out together that one time, and I'm not about to repeat it. Whatever we once had was good, but it's over, finished."

She looked at him quizzically. "You can honestly say that, Rick? Isn't there any spark left between us?"

"If there is, Contessa, then we're going to let it die out by itself. You're married and I'm married. I'm not going to risk spoiling two perfectly good relationships so that you can have your little bit of fun and excitement. Do you understand?"

"If that's the way you want it."

"It is the way I want it. Go back to your husband and your children and leave me to get on with my life."

"Fine," she said. She tossed back her hair in annoyance and strode off in the direction of the main house. Rick sighed with relief as he went to have the cases of rum loaded onto his truck. He felt pleased with himself. He had faced temptation and resisted it. Grace would be proud of him, except, of course, that he could never tell her.

Contessa strode in through the main door of Plantation House.

"Oh, Contessa, there you are," Marigot called. "Maman is waiting to serve lunch."

"Damn lunch," Contessa said. "Damn everybody."

She ran up the stairs and shut herself in her room.

"Damn Rick," she said to herself. Why did he have to turn so damned virtuous suddenly? What hold could that woman have over him? She was a nothing. There was no way he could prefer Grace to the incredible lovemaking he and Contessa had shared. It wasn't that she wanted to leave Robert and go back to Rick, but she liked the idea that he was there, across the island, pining for her, waiting for her to come to spice up his life every now and then.

"He'll be sorry," she thought, biting her lip to keep from crying. She refused to cry over Rick Sommers.

A few days later Grace felt well enough to drive into town. She had looked in the mirror and decided that she had resembled a ghost long enough. No wonder her husband was looking elsewhere for excitement. His own wife looked washed-out and unappealing. She'd drive down to the stores and buy herself some new outfits. There wasn't a maternity store in Marigot, but there were some chic boutiques and she was sure she could find something fashionable.

In a little shop called Panache she found a long hand-woven dress imported from Greece. She was just about to try it on, when Contessa walked into the store.

"Good heavens, it's poor little Grace, up and around again," she said. "How brave of you."

"Hello, Contessa," Grace said, and turned back to her purchase, holding it up against herself to see the effect.

"I wouldn't bother right now, honey," Contessa said. "It's hardly worth spending the money, when you never go anywhere or do anything."

Grace turned her cool gaze on Contessa's animated face. "I think you must have come into the wrong place, Contessa," she said. "The touristy shops are across the street. That's where they have all the bright, tacky clothes you like to wear. This is a boutique for people with taste— not you at all, I'm afraid."

Contessa flushed. "Your husband doesn't seem to have any complaints about the way I look," she said.

"Yes, well, all men are rather stupid when it comes to breast size," Grace said. "I doubt he notices what you've got on around them — since they're usually half hanging out anyway."

Contessa's eyes flashed dangerously. "I don't usually keep whatever I'm wearing on long enough for him to notice," she said. "In any case, he keeps coming back for more."

"Keep dreaming, Contessa," Grace said.

Contessa gave her a long, pitying smile. "Darling, why do you think he has to make all those little trips up to Paradise Rum?" she said. "You really are a sweet, naive person, aren't you? We usually ship orders direct to our clients. They don't have to come pick them up in person ... unless they have another reason for coming up to see us."

"You're lying, Contessa," Grace said.

"You don't believe me?" Contessa said. "Why don't you ask Rick what happened when we went riding? Riding is such wonderful exercise, don't you think? And Rick is such an exercise fiend ... he can never seem to get enough .... "

"Just get out of here and take your ugly lies with you," Grace said. "If you weren't such a little tramp, you'd make sure your own husband and children were happy and stop trying to take what doesn't belong to you."

Contessa paused dramatically, as if she were considering something, then she said, "Maybe that's another reason Rick can't seem to stay away from me. Maybe blood is thicker than water, as they say."

"What are you talking about?" Grace demanded.

Contessa raised an eyebrow. She moved closer to Grace. "Have you ever noticed my little Anthony's smile? When he smiles he has the most adorable little dimple, right here …." She pointed to her cheek. "Someone else I know has a smile just like that. Maybe you know him, Grace."

Grace flung the dress down on the counter. "I've heard enough of this garbage," she said. "You should take up writing, Contessa. You're really very good at making up cheap, trashy stories!"

She swept past Contessa and got into her car, her tires screeching as she drove away. Instead of taking the direct route home, she swung to the left, along the cliff-top road. She wouldn't go back to the hotel at all. She'd go to her cottage until she'd regained her composure. She just wanted to be alone, to feel the wind rushing in her face and to blot out the fears that were threatening to engulf her. She hadn't let Contessa see how much she was getting to her, at least she was glad of that, but now that she was alone, the taunting words sang in her head. The trouble was that she suspected everything Contessa said had been true. Rick was still carrying a torch for her. He was still seeing her whenever he could, and he'd always love her more! Maybe Anthony was his son, the son he so desperately wanted when she could provide him only with a daughter!

Grace began to drive faster and faster. Suddenly the road in front of her swung unexpectedly inland. She found herself heading straight for the cliff top. With all her strength she wrenched the wheel and the car came around on two tires. A little voice of reason inside her head warned her to slow down, but she didn't even care anymore. It didn't matter what happened to her if she didn't have Rick's love. She didn't care about anything. She just wanted to get away. How could she ever live on the same island as Contessa knowing that she'd never be free of her, knowing that she'd always have to watch her gloating face as Rick ran back to her again and again ….

She was driving through a wild scrubland area now. Goats and sheep grazed behind stone walls. Stunted pine bent against the force of the wind. The road zigzagged beside impressive cliffs. She passed through a hamlet with a couple of red-roofed houses, a few banana trees, and goats. As she came out the other side of the village, a herd of goats emerged from a gate directly in front of her, driven by a little boy no more than eight years old. In horror Grace swung the wheel to avoid them. The car swerved out of control, hit a rock, and then flew out, over the cliff. For a second it seemed to hang there, with time and motion suspended, then it plunged from sight, landing in a fiery explosion on the rocks below.

CHAPTER 18

C ontessa came home early from town. The scene
with Grace had taken away her enthusiasm for
shopping. She was just beginning a solitary lunch
when Robert walked in.

"Sorry. I got hungry and started without you," she said,
looking up from her salad.

"I'm surprised you have an appetite after a tragedy like
this morning's," he said.

She looked up, an artichoke heart speared to her fork.
"Tragedy, what tragedy?"

"You haven't heard? It's all over the island and I
assumed— Oh, my poor sweetheart, I'm so sorry. What a
shock for you." He came over and took her hand. "Grace
Sommers's car went over a cliff …."

He was still talking, but Contessa couldn't hear what he
was saying because of the blood pounding through her
head and ringing in her ears. She opened her mouth and a
great sob shook her whole body. Immediately Robert put
his arm around her. "Honey, don't cry. It's okay," he said.

She shook her head, trying to form words. "No, it's not
okay. You don't understand," she blurted out. "I did it. It's
all my fault!"

"What are you talking about, sweetheart?" Robert's voice was still soothing. "Of course it wasn't your fault. They said she was alone and driving very fast when it happened."

Contessa shook her head. "It was my fault, Robert. I said some terrible things to her. I upset her so much that she drove over a cliff." Tears began cascading down her cheeks as her body convulsed from crying.

"What did you say to her?" Robert's voice was suddenly sharp.

"I made fun of her, I guess," she said between sobs. "I told her that her husband preferred me to her ...."

"Why would you do a thing like that, Contessa?"

She looked down hopelessly at the table. Why had she behaved like that? What was there in Grace Sommers that brought out this dark side in her? "She started it," she said. "She put me down the very first time we met. And every time since. Every time I've tried to be friends, she's snubbed me and made me feel small. I just wanted to get back at her ... but I didn't want her dead, I swear."

"She's not dead," Robert said flatly.

"You said her car went over a cliff."

"It did, but she was very lucky. She was thrown out as it flipped and she landed in a bush just below the road. She's in the hospital in Philipsburg. They think she's going to be okay."

"And the baby?"

"I don't know about the baby."

There was a silence while Contessa tried to control the wild extremes of emotion raging through her. She had gone through shock, incredible guilt, and then the anger that comes with relief. She was angry at Robert for letting her think that Grace was dead, and for then tricking her into a confession, because that was how it now seemed to her. She was also scared because Robert's face was hard and suspicious as he looked at her. It wasn't the adoring face she was used to. She wondered if she had gone too far this time. Robert was so possessive with her. He wouldn't be likely to understand or forgive any flirtation with Rick.

"Why are you looking at me like that?" she demanded, wriggling uncomfortably under his gaze.

"This nonsense about you and Rick Sommers?" he demanded. "It is just nonsense, isn't it? Just the sort of catty thing women say to each other?"

Contessa tossed her head. "Of course it's nonsense," she said. "Why would you think otherwise?"

Robert was continuing to frown at her. "There must be something to it, or Grace would never have believed any of it."

Contessa looked down at the tablecloth. "Okay, if you really must know, Rick Sommers has been pestering me," she said. "He carried a torch for me while I waited for you to come back to the island, and it seems he's never gotten over me. I told him long ago, there's only one man for me, but he still never misses a chance to come up to the plantation with hopes of seeing me for a moment …."

A spasm of fury crossed Robert's face. "Has he touched you? Because if he has, I'll—"

"Do you think I've given him the chance?" she said haughtily. "You have to understand that Rick likes beautiful women. It's only natural that he's still attracted to me, but you need not worry, darling. I'm interested in only one man, and always will be."

She patted his hand, but he snatched it away.

"Where are you going?" she demanded.

"Down to Sommers's hotel to teach him a lesson he won't forget," Robert said.

Contessa leapt up from the table. Her knife clattered to the floor and a servant rushed to pick it up. "Robert, no, please," Contessa begged. She grabbed his arm. "Don't do anything to make more trouble, I beg of you. Rick has had his punishment. He's nearly lost his wife. Maybe he's lost his baby. He won't bother me again, I can guarantee."

Robert looked down at her with tenderness. "You're a good person, my darling," he said, "and maybe you're right. No good can come of fighting, although I have to tell you I have an irresistible urge to tear him apart. But I'm not going to let him get away with this …." He stared out of the window, across the sweeping lawns.

"What are you going to do?" Contessa asked in a small voice.

"Something that's been in the back of my mind for some time," he said. "You probably don't know this, Contessa, but we hold the lease on Trade Winds' land. Now that it's doing so well, I think it's time to do something about that lease. You wouldn't mind a half share in Trade Winds, would you, darling?"

Contessa ran the picture through her head. She saw herself welcoming rich and famous guests, maybe telling Grace Sommers what to do …. "I wouldn't mind it at all," she said.

"I'm going to take a look at that lease right now," Robert said. "The old man drew it up when we were kids, and I've never studied it in detail. Maybe there's a way to get our hands on the property."

He strode down the hall and into his father's study. He opened what he thought was the correct drawer in the file cabinet, rummaged through it, and then frowned.

"What are you looking for, Robert?" His father's voice behind him made him jump.

Robert stood up. "The deed to Trade Winds' land, Father. I thought you always kept it in here," Robert said.

"The deed to Trade Winds," Christof said slowly. "What would you want with that?"

"Just to take a look at it, see the terms and conditions. Any idea where it might have gone?"

Christof cleared his throat. "Yes. I don't have it anymore."

"Who does?"

"Rick Sommers."

"Rick? How did he get it?"

"I gave it to him."

"You gave the Trade Winds deed back to Rick? Father, why? How could you do that without consulting us?" Robert stormed.

Christof held up his hand. "Just a minute before you go shooting your mouth off. I had no choice about the deed. It seemed like the only thing to do to keep Paradise Rum intact."

"What are you talking about, Father? Why didn't you have a choice?"

Christof sighed. "I suppose it has to come out some-time," he said. "I thought I'd spare you from all the unpleasant details, but you have a right to know." He paused and ran his hand through his iron-gray hair. He had been dreading this moment, but the story he had invented seemed the only solution. "Right after the plane crash and the funeral I was approached by a Miami lawyer represent-ing Rick. He told me they were going to sue. It was my plane, you see, my pilot, my idea to go to St. Barts .... The lawyer was prepared to go after Paradise Rum ... the puni-tive damages could have run into the millions ...."

Robert's face was furious. "How could Rick do such a thing to us? You've always treated him like your own son—better than your own sons."

"I don't blame Rick, " Christof said. "You saw him yourself. He was in a state of shock at the time. I don't think he had a clue as to what was going on. I'm sure the lawyer latched on to him, probably scared him by telling him how easily he could lose everything if he weren't care-ful. Everything his parents worked for would be for noth-ing. Rick was in a vulnerable state. He would have agreed to anything. I had to think fast, Robert. I came up with the idea of the deed. Rick agreed to drop the lawsuit if I gave him the deed to Trade Winds. To my mind it was a small price to pay."

"A small price? Father, that's prime land."

"What use would it be to us?"

"Land is always valuable. We might need to expand our sugarcane production in the near future."

"It's not good cane land, as you well know. Too salty."

"Maybe not, but it's a prime site. We might have wanted to go into the hotel business someday."

Christof put his large hand on his son's shoulder. "Forget about it, Robert. We are making all the money we need from rum. There are plenty of other properties in the Caribbean if you want to invest. Leave Rick Sommers his own little corner. It seems to me that the deed to a few acres of land was a poor trade for the loss of both his parents."

"I don't see it like that," Robert snapped. "I see that Rick Sommers took advantage of us and continues to take advantage of us."

"How so?"

"It doesn't matter."

"I don't understand you, Robert. His wife barely escaped death today ... do you wish disaster on him at a time like this?"

"He brought that on himself too," Robert said, "but I don't want to talk about it. If the deed is gone, then it's gone, and we can't get it back. But I won't forget. Rick Sommers owes us, Father. We'll get even sometime."

"Robert, Robert!" Christof said. "You've always been jealous of Rick, haven't you? When you were young, you always complained that I liked him more than you. Well, you're a man now. You should have outgrown such childishness long ago. Be thankful for what you have and let Rick enjoy what he has too. I don't like what I've been seeing lately. There's a rift growing between our two families, and it upsets me. On a small island like this we need to get along—so no more pettiness? Understand?" Robert didn't answer, so he repeated more forcefully, "I said, understand?"

"Yes, Father," Robert muttered, and pushed past Christof to leave the study.

Grace Sommers floated toward the surface of consciousness from the deep dark region of twisted dreams where she had spent the last few hours. Somewhere above her, a voice was chanting. It was a pleasant, soothing voice, and she tried to place it, wondering where it belonged in her dream. Slowly the words began to make sense to her.

"Gracie, please don't die. Please come back, Gracie. I love you. I love you so much. I can't live without you. I need you. Ellen needs you …."

With difficulty she opened her eyes, blinking from the bright light around her. Rick was sitting beside her, holding her hand and gazing down at her with imploring eyes.

"Rick?" she managed to whisper.

"Grace? Thank God. I was so afraid I'd lost you." Tears started to trickle down his cheeks. "When I saw the car, all twisted and burned at the bottom of the cliff, I thought it was all over. I didn't want to go on living without you. And then they found you in that bush. It was like a miracle, Grace."

Grace put a hand up to her face and touched bandages. She was just beginning to remember: driving very fast and the little boy had stepped out with the goats and the car was spinning out of control right toward the cliff ….

"I was going over the cliff," she said.

"The car did," Rick said. "Luckily it hit a rock first and you were thrown out. You landed in a big bush that broke your fall. The doctor says that you're fine, apart from cuts and bruises."

"And the baby?"

Rick squeezed her hand. "As far as they can tell, no harm done." He took out his handkerchief and blew his nose. "God, Grace, what were you doing, driving so fast on that road?"

Painful memories were coming back. "I just wanted to escape," she said.

"From what?"

"From everything Contessa told me about the two of you."

Rick's eyes narrowed. "What did Contessa tell you?"

"That you still preferred her to me. That you kept making trips up to Paradise Rum just to see her. She even said ... that Anthony was your son."

"And you believed all that nonsense?"

"I didn't know what to believe," she said. "It all seemed to add up. I saw you out riding with her, Rick, and you lied about it. I knew you'd been up to Paradise Rum. And I knew I hadn't been much of a wife to you lately."

"Grace, listen to me." He took both her hands in his. "Whatever happened between me and Contessa was over long ago, before I met you. She might want to revive it, but I told her I wasn't interested. I know I haven't always been true to one woman, but I swear to you that I haven't been with anyone else since we married. Do you believe me?"

She looked into his eyes, then she nodded. "Yes, Rick, I believe you," she said.

"I want you to trust me, whatever Contessa says, " he

said. "Twisting the truth is just another way of spicing up a life she finds rather boring at the moment. She's a dangerous woman, Grace. We'll make sure we both stay away from her in the future. Next time I'll send Samuel up to Paradise Rum."

"Oh, Rick," Grace said, tears of relief trickling down her cheeks. "I can't believe how dumb I was. I should have just asked you, but I thought that what she said could so easily be true. I haven't been able to share your life lately. I really thought that I wasn't much of a wife to you at the moment, looking the way I do, lying there sick and useless."

Rick took her face gently in his hands. "I didn't marry you just for the good times, Grace," he said. "Anyone can be loving and faithful when things are going well. I promised to love you in sickness and in health, and I do. Besides, I am partly to blame for your present condition. After this one, no more babies for a while. We need to start enjoying life again. Right?"

Grace nodded. "I suppose there's no truth to what she said about Anthony being your son?"

"Like I said, she has to find ways to spice up her life," he whispered. He realized that it was all too possible that Anthony was his child. He also realized that no good could come of admitting the truth. He had his own little family now, and Robert adored Anthony. Better to pretend the past had never happened. "Let her say what she likes," he added. "She can't harm us."

She squeezed his hand. "I feel sorry for Contessa," she said, "if her life is so boring that she has to try to stir up trouble for other people."

Rick raised a warning finger. "We are not going to discuss Contessa ever again. She is a taboo subject in the Sommers household. Let the Philipses get on with their rum making and we're going to concentrate on our kids and our hotel and each other!"

He bent carefully toward her and kissed her gently on the lips. Grace closed her eyes and lay back with a sigh of contentment.

Up at Plantation House Contessa was lying down after lunch, when Robert stormed in, slamming the door behind him.

She sat up in alarm. "What is it? What's the matter, darling?"

"Wait until you hear what I've just discovered," he said, hardly able to talk through his anger. "My father had to turn over the lease to Rick Sommers to save the expense of a lawsuit."

"Rick was going to sue your father? I can't believe it," Contessa said.

"I know, I couldn't believe it either, but it shows you the kind of man he is: pretending to be best friends with my father and my family and at the same time stabbing us in the back. He may have his hands on our land, but I swear to God, if he tries to get his hands on my wife again, I'll kill him."

Contessa rose up, alarmed at the look on his face. The whole thing had gone too far. She put a restraining hand on Robert's shoulder. "Don't talk like that, Robert. You know what Rick's like with women. It probably meant nothing to him—and you certainly don't have to worry about me. I'm your devoted wife and I won't let anything spoil our marriage. Let's forgive and forget, okay?"

Robert shook himself free of her hand. "I don't know if I can either forgive or forget," he said. "He's not to be trusted, Contessa. We're going to make sure that we stay well away from the Sommerses in the future. Father can plan all the happy family gatherings he wants, but you and I are not going to be there."

CHAPTER 19

Christof pushed the throttle of his powerful Tiara forward and skimmed over the smooth surface of the sea. He stood at the wheel, savoring the wind in his hair, the salt on his lips, and the surge of his boat's speed and power. The boat had always been his great escape whenever he felt weighed down by the pressures of life, but he had hardly been out on it at all since … Christof closed his eyes to shut out the tragedy that still hurt too much to think about. He missed Ingrid with a hurt that left him in physical pain. He had always been a positive thinker, a man of action. He had disapproved of Nazi Germany, and when he couldn't stop the madness, he left. He had wanted a better quality rum than could be bought in local stores, so he produced his own. He knew that he should put the past behind him and get on with his life. He had two sons who were already great assets to his business. Will had come up with new ways to combat pests in the cane fields and increase the crop yield. Robert's tireless efforts brought in new accounts every month. He had two healthy grandsons. That was a lot to be thankful for, he knew. But he had nobody to share his dreams or his fears with …. He would have given anything to discuss what was troubling him at the moment: the growing rift between Robert's family and the Sommerses. He could sense the resentment festering in Robert, out of proportion to the small matter of a deed. He had no idea that his little white lie could cause so much trouble. Robert was able to buy any land that struck his fancy. Paradise Rum had insured that. Why, then, was he so obsessed with losing the deed to a few choice acres? There was still lots of beach-front property on the island. Christof wished he could find a way to heal the wounds of those he loved best, but he didn't know how. He hoped that taking to the water would help put things in perspective.

About five miles from land he cut the engine and threw out the anchor. He hadn't brought diving equipment with him today—in fact he hadn't been down since that fateful dive—but he always carried his mask and flippers in the bottom of the boat. The blue water called to him, and he pulled the flippers on impatiently before slipping down over the side of the boat. At the last moment he reached for his spear gun and started out along the surface, moving in an easy, graceful motion.

Within half an hour he had speared a good-size rainbow runner and a gray snapper, both of which would be delicious when grilled over coals later. That was enough for one day, he decided. He never took more than he could eat. As he climbed back into the boat, he stiffened. A boat, sails flapping idly, seemed to be drifting right over the area where the wreck of La Targa lay. A chill began to spread over Christof. He must get over there and warn them of the danger! He hoped he was not already too late.

Earlier that day, Grace Sommers had awoken feeling completely well for the first time in her eight months of pregnancy. She climbed out of bed full of energy and ready for anything her large girth would allow. Ever since her life had been handed back to her on the cliff top, each day seemed like a new miracle to be enjoyed. Rick was more loving and attentive than he had ever been. Ellen was now walking and beginning to talk, changing from baby into delightful child. And, as Samuel had predicted, she was already wrapping her father around her little finger. When Ellen held up her arms and said "Daddy" in her clear little voice, Grace could see Rick's eyes mist over as he scooped her up and set her upon his shoulders. She wondered what difference a second child would make. This second child who had survived against all odds was a fighter. Grace suddenly felt a sharp kick against her belly, as if the baby knew what she was thinking.

Grace went about her morning chores charged with energy. She changed the flower arrangements in the public areas, checked out several guests, and went over the lunch menu. Then she sought out Rick, who she found frowning over accounts.

"I've got a great idea," she said. "Let's go sailing."

He looked up and laughed. "You're crazy."

"What's so crazy about going sailing?" she said.

"Several things. For one—you are the size of a house, and two, we are running a hotel."

Grace perched on the corner of his desk. "I've just checked out this morning's departures. The new guests won't be in until the afternoon plane, and lunch is taken care of. It's a perfectly calm day without a cloud in the sky. There would be no more danger sitting in a boat than there would sitting here."

"I don't know, Grace," Rick said doubtfully.

"Rick, I haven't been sailing since way before Ellen was born, and I don't think you've been out for the longest time either. Remember how we used to love sailing together when we first met? Let's just go out for an hour or so."

"If you really think it's okay," Rick said.

"I do think it's okay," Grace insisted. She half dragged him from his seat. "Come on, you're wasting precious time."

"Grace, wait a minute. We can't just leave the hotel."

"I've already talked to Samuel and Dumas. Everything is covered," she said. "I want to do it for you more than for me. I've been worried that you don't get any free time anymore."

"That's the price of success, I suppose," he said.

"But you're the sort of person who needs to play," she said.

"You're saying I haven't grown up yet?" he teased.

"All men are just big kids at heart," she said, smiling fondly at him. "Some more than others. You've had to give up all the activities you used to love—" She paused and hit him because he was grinning. "Not that sort of activity. I mean boating and diving—outdoor stuff—and I'm going to see that it becomes part of your life again. Starting now."

"I can tell you're fully recovered," Rick said. "You're back to your old bossy self."

"You better believe it," Grace said, laughing as she took his hand.

There was a light breeze blowing down from the island,

but the sea was completely calm. Rick let out the sail and they eased away from the dock, steering past the moored pleasure crafts and guests on pedalos and air beds. When they were clear of the bay, the breeze stiffened, sending them through the water at a good speed. Grace glanced at Rick, sitting in the stern, tiller in hand. Already he looked more relaxed than he had in months, and she felt wonderful. The wind in her face was fresh and cool. Flying fish rose up in front of them, making her cry out with delight. She stood up in the bow to watch as they leapt free of the water and flew through the air before disappearing again.

"Some figurehead you'd make," Rick teased. "I can't see around you."

"How rude!" she said, and moved to kneel on the bench. "Don't you dare say anything about my weight upsetting the balance of the boat."

"I wasn't going to, but come to think of it, we are a little low in the water," he said.

She leaned over the side to flick water up at him, not knowing he was planning to come about at that moment. As she cautiously leaned forward, the boat changed course and she slammed up against the side of the boat. Rick saw it happen and instantly corrected course.

"Grace honey? Are you all right?" he called.

"Yes, just a little shook up," she said. "Next time you're going to change course, don't do it when I'm leaning out of the boat."

"I'm sorry. I thought you were ready," Rick said. "Are you sure you're okay? Do you think we should go back?"

"No, no. I'm fine," she said, "and I don't want to go back

yet. I'll probably have a bruise tomorrow, but I'm sure the baby is fine. He's well cushioned against bumps like that."

"Maybe you'd better sit down from now on," Rick said. Then, as she continued to stand, "Grace, I really think it would be a good idea if you sat down, just in case …."

"Rick," she said in a tight voice, "I don't think I am fine … There's water running down my legs."

"What?"

"My waters have broken. Oh, God. I'd better sit down."

"Grace?" His hand still on the tiller, Rick stared at her in disbelief.

"I'm going into labor, Rick. I think you'd better come up here. "

"Now? Grace, you can't go into labor now. You've got another couple of weeks to go."

"Tell that to the baby," she said. "It seems to think that … whoa!" She clutched at her stomach, her face clenched in pain.

"What is it?" Rick cried in alarm.

"A contraction, genius," she said when she could breathe again.

"I'll get you back to land," Rick said. "Just sit tight and I'll bring us around."

Grace looked out at the island. It seemed very far away. She noticed the sail flapping. The breeze had dropped into the lee of the mountains. She braced herself as the next contraction began. Holding on to the side of the boat for support, she breathed deeply as wave after wave of pain flowed over her.

"Rick!" she called in alarm as soon as it was over.

"Remember how long it took to have Ellen?"

"Yeah. Not very long. She just sort of popped out."

"I think this one is going to do the same."

"You mean now? Here?"

She nodded. "I don't think I'm going to make it back to land. Get over here now and help me."

There was panic in his eyes. "God, Grace, I can't deliver a baby. I don't know anything about it."

"You don't have to know anything," she yelled as the pain started to overtake her again. "It's coming by itself. I can feel it, Rick. Help me!"

In a flash he was at her side and eased her down onto the floor of the boat. "It's okay, honey," he said, holding her hand. "It's going to be okay. Just relax."

"I think you're the one who should relax," she snapped. She closed her eyes again, squeezing his hand and gasping desperately. "Now, Rick, now," she panted. "It's coming now!"

He lifted her skirt and saw the head and face of his new baby emerge. "One more push, honey," he said as he held on to the baby's shoulders. Grace gritted her teeth, and suddenly Rick found himself staring down into the dark blue eyes of a scowling baby boy. He wriggled in his father's arms, opened his mouth, and gave a loud, protesting cry. Rick stood looking down in amazement, as if he didn't believe he had just helped deliver his own child.

"Is it okay?" Grace asked weakly. "What is it?"

Rick looked up at her, his face a picture of ecstasy. "It's a little boy and he's perfect," he said.

Christof climbed aboard his boat and threw off his mask and flippers. He trained his binoculars on a drifting sailboat in the distance. What he saw made him stiffen with apprehension. He recognized the boat and could easily make out Rick Sommers's fair hair. He was leaning over the side of the boat, attempting to drag something out of the water.

Savagely Christof started the engine and opened the throttle. The speedboat responded and a sheet of water flew up on either side as he raced toward them. When he was close enough he cut the motor.

"Rick, what are you doing?" he yelled in a panic.

"Come and see," Rick yelled back, a big grin on his face.

Christof drifted closer, then his eyes opened wide in amazement. The object Rick was holding in the water was a newborn baby.

"He seems to like it," Rick explained, looking up at Christof with pride all over his face. "He wouldn't stop bawling after he was born until I put him in the ocean to wash him off. Then he just stopped and he's quite content to stay in the water."

"Your baby?" Christof was confused. "I didn't know Grace had the baby."

"About ten minutes ago," Rick said.

"Out here? On the boat?"

Grace managed to raise her head. "That's right, Christof. In the boat. We Sommerses don't do anything conventionally."

"Grace? How are you feeling?"

"Overjoyed! And tired. But I'm fine. Rick was just cleaning him off before we took him home, but he seems to like the water."

Christof admired the sturdy little limbs, the dark eyes

and hair. "A baby boy. My sincere congratulations to you both. What are you going to call him?"

"Ocean," Rick said. "It seemed appropriate."

"Ocean Sommers," Christof said. "He certainly seems like a child of the sea. Quite unique. It's almost as if he's smiling. Maybe he'll be the one."

"The one for what, Christof?" Rick asked.

"To heal the rift. To bring the families back together again," Christof said. "There is no place for bad feeling on this island, and I love you all. It hurts me to see our families at odds like this." Then he checked himself as if he were ashamed of saying so much. "If you throw me a line, I'll tow you back to shore. These two should be checked out by a doctor, although they both seem to be in great shape …."

Rick handed the baby to Grace, who held him close to her, stroking the dark fuzz of hair and kissing the top of his head. Christof started the engine and gently pulled the sail-boat in the direction of the shore. St. Martin came closer and closer, its shaggy mountain glowing in the bright light of midday. Trade Winds stood proud and elegant on the shore. Grace looked at it with joy in her heart.

"Look, Ocean, we're almost home," she murmured to the baby.

THE END
AND THE BEGINNING

COMING NEXT!
THE SECRETS OF
LAKE SUCCESS!

Will a beautiful young woman find
happiness or treachery when she inherits
her father's company? Will her efforts to
save her family cost her the love of the
one man she adores? Find out all the
mysteries of this small town when you
read the newest Great Escapes novel, and
watch the miniseries on-air!

ON NBC
THIS OCTOBER—
THE SECRETS OF LAKE SUCCESS